D0833891

Amor Eterno

Amor Eterno

Eleven Lessons in Love

Patricia Preciado Martin

The University of Arizona Press   Tucson

∞ This book is printed on acid-free, archival-quality paper.
Manufactured in the United States of America

05 04 03 02 01 00   6 5 4 3 2 1

Library of Congress Cataloging-in-Publication Data

Martin, Patricia Preciado.
Amor eterno: eleven lessons in love / Patricia Preciado Martin.
p. cm. –(Camino del sol)
ISBN 0-8165-1994-3 (alk. paper)–ISBN 0-8165-1995-1 (pbk.: alk.
paper)
1. Mexican Americans—Social life and customs—
Fiction. 2. Love stories, American. I. Title. II. Series.
PS3563.A7272 A83 2000
813'.54–dc21   99-006918

British Library Cataloguing-in-Publication Data
A catalogue record for this book is available from the British
Library.

Publication of this book is made possible in part by the proceeds of
a permanent endowment created with the assistance of a Challenge
Grant from the National Endowment for the Humanities, a federal
agency.

Dedicated to my husband, Jim,

amigo, compañero, esposo, amante, padre, amor eterno

Contents

Amor de Acuerdo—Arranged Love 1

Amor Perdido—Lost Love 9

Amor Sufrido—Long-Suffering Love 19

Amor de Madre—Mother's Love 27

Amor Prohibido—Forbidden Love 41

Amor Desesperado—Desperate Love 51

Amor Encantado—Enchanted Love 61

Amor Frustrado—Frustrated Love 71

Amor e Ilusión—Love and Illusion 77

Amor Inolvidable—Unforgettable Love 87

Amor Eterno—Eternal Love 97

Acknowledgments

I am indebted, as always, to more friends, relatives, and antepasados than I can name. Indeed many of the names of these who have inspired me I do not know—but they are the people who have passed down the stories. Gracias, especially, to my husband Jim and our children, Elena and Jim, who are always my patient first audience and my most gracious reviewers. I am grateful to the Mexican American community of Tucson and Arizona and El Norte who have planted the seeds for so many cuentos. In particular, gracias to Frank Valadéz, an amigo from Chicago whose family story is the inspiration for "Amor Perdido." Muchísimas gracias also to Teresa Flores and Ruben Moreno for recounting the stories of their mothers' devotions during the Korean War; I have tried to honor all our madrecitas with the story "Amor de Madre." Ruben wrote the letters that appear in the aforementioned story, and his firsthand war experience as well as his considerable writing talent and input have given the story an authenticity I could not have accomplished otherwise. My thanks to my editor, Patti Hartmann, who reacted so positively to my unfinished manuscript and encouraged me to continue writing the collection. Her ideas and suggestions, without a single exception, were always on the mark. Thanks also to my manuscript editors, Alexis Mills Noebels and Judith Allen, who were so patient and flexible. And gracias to all the staff at the University of Arizona Press who have participated in all the many processes of publishing a book. No small labor of love, indeed.

Amor de Acuerdo :: Arranged Love

QUIZÁS, QUIZÁS, QUIZÁS
O. Farrés

Siempre que te pregunto
Que cómo, cuándo y dónde,
Tú siempre me respondes,
Quizás, quizás, quizás.
Y así pasan los días
Y yo desesperado
Y tú, tú contestando,
Quizás, quizás, quizás.
Estás perdiendo el tiempo
Pensando, pensando
Por lo que tú más quieras
Hasta cuando, hasta cuando.
Y así pasan los días
Y yo desesperado
Y tú, tú contestando,
Quizás, quizás, quizás.

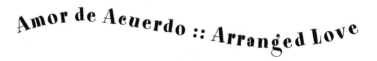

Amor de Acuerdo :: Arranged Love

21 de abril, 1878
Hacienda de
Bacadehuachi
Pinos Altos, Chihuahua,
México

My most widely esteemed Don Ignacio Rascón García:

I am writing to you these humble lines and am asking you, on behalf of myself and my spouse, Doña Telésfora Villa, for your kind disposition to forgive me my brashness and lack of modesty in therefore addressing myself to you for the first time and without proper introduction, but I assure you that I do so in the fulfillment of my obligation as a father—an obligation which all fathers must meet as given by the law of God—that is to say, to give credence to the

state of our sons after their indoctrination in the Holy
Catholic Faith.

Be that as it may, our son, Exiquio Jesús, has found it of
proper timing to fulfill the seventh of the Sacraments of
Our Holy Mother Church—that is so to say, Matrimony—
and for his companion in life he has selected with prayerful
hopefulness your daughter, Mercedes María, to whom he
was formerly introduced at the solemn fiesta of Nuestro
Señor de Esquipulas, the patron of the Hacienda de la
Buena Vista, by your nephew, her primo hermano,
Feliciano de la Cruz. Our son, Exiquio Jesús, was quite
taken with your daughter's comeliness, modesty, and wit,
and in compliance with my duty, I hope and pray that you,
as well as your highly regarded wife, Doña Socorro Vigil, as
well as the chosen of my son, will take our plea into prayerful account and consideration and give us your eagerly
awaited reply in the most brevity possible.

I remain your most attentive servidor,
Don Gorgonio Romero Cárdenas

15 de mayo, 1898
Ciudad de Guerrero,
Chihuahua, México

My most highly esteemed and respected Don Gorgonio
Romero Cárdenas:

I have received your most respectful letter with the
greatest honor and humility requesting the hand of our
daughter, Mercedes María, to be joined in Holy Matrimony
with that of your son and heir, Exiquio Jesús. I hasten to
assure you that it would be an immeasurable blessing for

our humble family to be thus joined with such an illustrious and renowned house as yours.

I am therefore bereaved to inform you that in spite of our reasoning and cajoling—and, indeed, devout supplications to San Antonio—our daughter Mercedes María is obstinate in her refusal to acquiesce to this most fortuitous of arrangements.

We beg your kind patience in this most embarrassing of situations. We hasten to add that we are most concerned about our only daughter: she paces and laments; she refuses solid nourishment; she keeps continual vigilance at the window of the sala for what or whom we do not know. We trust that you and your son will understand that we are doing everything in our power—including enlisting the counsel and persuasive powers of the monseñor from the basilica de Santa Marta de las Cuevas. We are hopeful that she will soon come to her senses and agree to submit to her destiny to join in this most blessed and fortuitous of unions.

I remain your most respectful and humble servidor,
Don Ignacio Rascón García

25 de septiembre, 1898
Hacienda de
Bacadehuachi
Pinos Altos, Chihuahua,
México

Estimado Don Ignacio Rascón García:

It was with great sorrow and a heavy heart that we received your letter in which you informed us of the reluctance of your daughter, Mercedes María, to agree to the betrothal arrangements with our son Exiquio Jesús. I beg your indulgence for the delay in my response, but I will confide that we have also been vigilant and concerned about the emotional and spiritual state of our only son and heir. For a time he has been quite despondent and lacking in interest in attending to his duties as the mayordomo of our hacienda. He has become listless about pursuing his favorite pastimes—playing his guitar, attending the charreadas on días de fiestas, and playing cards with his friends at Ranchos de Santiago. But I have become more optimistic since he has relied on the advice of my uncle, His Excellency Bishop Demetrio Rojas, from the cathedral of our fair capital. Exiquio Jesús is presently making a pilgrimage and novena to Magdalena, Sonora, for the feast day of San Francisco on the fourth of October accompanied by my brother, Don Ildelfonso Cárdenas (and incidentally, your nephew Feliciano de la Cruz, who is rumored to be lovesick himself with a secret infatuation). Exiquio's intention is to plead to that most miraculous and tenderhearted of saints that his desire to be wed to Mercedes María be fulfilled. We are awaiting his return heartened and hopeful and are anxiously waiting further communication with you regarding this most delicate of matters.

I remain in your debt,
Don Gorgonio Romero Cárdenas

17 de octubre, 1898
Ciudad de Guerrero,
Chihuahua, México

Estimado Don Gorgonio Romero Cárdenas:

I have received your most recent letter, and with great thanksgiving and gratitude, my wife and I have once again consulted with our daughter, Mercedes María, and thanks to the intercession of the benevolent San Francisco, she is now in agreement to sign the proposal for the marriage contract between her and your son, Exiquio Jesús. We now give you leave to make whatever arrangements that you deem necessary for the betrothal and marriage fiestas as required by our Holy Mother Church.

Our daughter brings into the matrimonial contract a humble dowry of ten gold pesetas, a lacquered cross of great antiquity, a leather trunk with a selection of hand-embroidered and crocheted linens, a set of talavera pottery, a featherbed mattress, twelve yearling calves, a palomino stallion and mare, a milk cow, a dozen hectares planted with corn and alfalfa, a herd of angora goats, and four dozen chickens.

As we are sure you must be aware, our daughter Mercedes María is famed for her beauty in the whole valley. She is orderly and abstemious in her personal habits and is not quarrelsome nor a complainer. She is literate—she can read and write and do her sums thanks to the good sisters of the Convento de Santa Clara. She plays the guitar and mandolin and is renowned for her beautiful singing voice. She is skilled in the arts of needlework, sewing, cooking, and recitations. She is pious, attending vigils and mass without complaint.

She is winsome and of a gentle character, and we are sure that she will be of great assistance, not only to her adoring spouse, but also to you and your wife and eight daughters in attending to domestic matters at your hacienda in the valley of Bacadehuachi.

We are at your disposition and await your word as to the time and place and requirements of the betrothal fiesta.

I remain your most humble servant,

Don Ignacio Rascón García

Amor Perdido :: Lost Love

ESTRELLITA

Manuel Ponce

Estrellita de lejano cielo
Que miras mi dolor
Que sabes mi sufrir
Baja y dime si me quiere un poco
Porque ya no puedo
Sin su amor vivir
Tú eres su estrella
El faro de mi amor
Tú sabes que pronto he de morir.
Baja y dime si me quiere un poco
Porque ya no puedo
Sin su amor vivir.

Amor Perdido :: Lost Love

(It was a memento that Francisco would dust off from time to time, remembering. He'd extract it carefully from a secret chamber of his heart, as if it were a delicate crystal heirloom, and hold it up to the continually diminishing light of the years that had passed. Like a kaleidoscope backlit by the sun, the slightest shift of his emotions would change the colors and the pattern, so that each time another design would emerge, each one more beautiful and fragile than the one that had preceded. And now that he had become a man and had loved and lost and loved again, he began to fully understand that the real meaning of his childhood journey to México, the land of his forefathers, would never be completely comprehended except by those who had themselves suffered the joys and the loss. . . .)

May 2, 1930
165 Escanaba Ave.
Chicago, Illinois

Don Lorenzo Villalpando
Unión de San Antonio, Jalisco, México

My dearest Tío Lorenzo:

I have been in communication of late with your compadre Don Domingo Morales, and he has informed me of his intention to make a journey to Unión de San Antonio in order to visit his ailing mother who is presently sequestered in the hospital of San Juan de Los Lagos. As you know so well, it is not possible for me at this time to return to México due to the political and personal circumstances of my husband's exile. But your compadre has generously extended an invitation to our youngest son, Francisco, that he might accompany him on his trip. We have agreed, although I must admit it is with some trepidation, and I prayerfully entrust him to your safekeeping.

It fills my heart with joy to know that our son will once again see the terreno of my ancestors, which is the foundation of our heritage and still the abode of my heart. I only ask of you one favor—that at sometime during his visit you take him to the family panteón in order that he may pay his respects to my beloved parents.

It is not propitious at this time that I regale you with the burdens of my life—suffice to say that my husband, Gerardo, has been injured in the steel mill, and I am now working seven days a week as a housekeeper and nursemaid for a wealthy americano family who live on the lake. It is so very fortuitous that my dear mother saw to it that I was

schooled in the domestic arts, as they have served me in
good stead during this time of hardship.

Un abrazo, que los quiero y los pienso,
Bentura Villalpando de Valadéz

Francisco had lived all the years of his short life on the
monotonous expanses of the "American" Midwest; the
south Chicago barrio where he had been born marked the
parameters of his daily world: the freezing winters and the
stifling summers, the skies dyed yellow by the belching steel
mills, and the poisoned, sluggish rivers. The crowded
apartment buildings with their darkened staircases and
sooty windows, the cracked sidewalks with their narrow
patches of browned grass, the aging school where pale
teachers attempted vainly to bleach out the stains of the
Mexican tongue and heart. His lullaby had been the
persistent rumbling of the trains. His playground was the
street, his starlight and moonlight the lamplight, his
greatest ambition and yearning the horizon of the city that
glittered falsely and beckoned nightly. . . .

On the first three days and nights of the long journey
to México, the train had steamed its way slowly in a south-
westerly direction across the flatlands and plains and deltas
of Middle America, crossing at last the high Mexican
deserts of Coahuila. Francisco had dozed intermittently,
entertained himself listlessly with his bag of toy cowboys
and Indians, played childish card games, and chatted
disinterestedly in his halting Spanish with his somber
elderly companion, hardly glancing out the sooty windows
of the passenger car. But then, when the engine began its
gargantuan effort to climb, traverse, and then descend the

enormous spine of the Sierra Madre Oriental, he began to kneel upright for a better view and to stare and exclaim with excitement. He had never seen mountains so high, mysterious, and blue, cloud-crowned at their summits like ancient gods. The valleys so deep and green, tattooed with the intricate terraces of maguey and maíz. Unexpected cataracts of crystalline waters tumbling down into secretive gorges. Deep and winding rivers, both languid and roaring. Bright flashes of brilliant birds embroidering the texture of the trees with their flight and song. Cascading flowers of every hue adorning the branches of the vines and trees: the San Miguelito, the bougainvilla, the jacaranda, and the flamboyant-red, like the color of his own pounding heart. He saw Spanish mustangs running free in pastures of saffron flowers. The mile after mile of stone corrals that embraced the land seemed to emerge from the earth without the intervention of man. Fields breathed long plumes of misty sighs in the clear, cool mornings. Tile-roofed hamlets exhaled a rosy haze with the setting sun. La tierra mexicana was ALIVE.

And when they arrived at long last at the bustling train station of San Juan de Los Lagos in the heart of Jalisco, México, they disembarked to begin their day's journey by horse and wagon to the remains of his ancestors' hacienda. And in the visages of the children peddling their mothers' quesadillas and tortas, he saw his own brown face and high cheekbones and burnished black hair—as if he were peering into the reflecting pool of an ancient sacrificial well. And in the basilica, where the pious compadre of his great-uncle had paused to light a candle in thanksgiving for the safe journey, he encountered the green-eyed Spanish features of his mother in the countenances of the devout women who were praying at the altar of the bejeweled and brocaded Virgin. And with the clear wisdom and vision of a child, he knew he had come home again. . . .

He spent the days of those unforgettable weeks at the side of a distant, fair-haired cousin from the pueblo, roaming the ruins of La Hacienda de la Buenaventura. What was the sorrow of his aged uncle and antepasados was the delight of the young boys and a source of high adventure and discovery: the surrounding high walls and enclosures, bullet-pocked and eroding. The crumbling chapel with the fallen hand-hewn beams that still smelled of smoke when it rained. The empty altar niches now harboring nests of colorful birds. The creaky, termite-ridden stairs to the empty bell tower, which had been plucked of its cast-iron bell and gaped like a toothless mouth. The weed-strewn family cemetery where the tumbled tombstones with exotic names scattered like so many spilled dominoes and where ancestors silently claimed their final meager heritage. The neglected corrales and gardens and orchards where desolate trees still bore fruit in their desperate struggle to survive. In the stone barns, still hanging in mournful disuse, were molding lariats woven of agave fibers and horsehair; chaparreras and saddlebags and sombreros and chalecos of aromatic sweat-stained leather stiffened with age; metal-studded saddles and bridles and spurs glinting in the half-light. It was here, in the abandoned horse stalls where the family's prize Arabians and quarter horses had stomped and snorted, that the swallows and long-nosed bats now reigned, flying heavenward in the gloomy dusk like souls on Judgement Day.

His great-uncle Lorenzo was a reflection of the grand old house—in ruins—his pale watery eyes clouded with the same ghosts that flitted in and out of the corridors. The mansion was in disrepair, only a few small rooms now used for habitation. The massive carved furniture in the great rooms was shrunken and dried under shrouds of dusty sheets. There were only empty silhouettes on the wall where gilded family portraits of saints and ancestors had hung. The sagging window shutters moaned their secrets with the slightest breeze. The patio was leaf strewn, its fountain filled with rubble. And rusted birdcages dangled in the porticoes empty of song. In the silence, the tiled corredores echoed the light footsteps of those who could not see the smoke of the burning fires on the horizon or the blood in the setting sun.

But Don Lorenzo—who had lost his inheritance and his family, now scattered across the vastness of El Norte like the dried leaves of autumn—had not lost his voice nor his memory. And at each day's end, by the light of the small fireplace in the former bedroom now used as a sala, the lonely old man entertained the boy with his recollections of the days of glory now gone by. The boy thrilled to the tales of bravery and horsemanship and charreadas and powerful Spanish mustangs; of music and bailes and fiestas and processions. Of great banquets and finery and beautiful women, his mother the fairest of all.

The boy, enthralled, would regale his tío, night after night, "Tell me again, Tío, the story of when my mother was Queen of the Charros."

Sovereign, lovely Mexican queen
who offers us her unequaled beauty,
here are your charros
who, brave and spirited,

come to sing to you today,
in their fiesta
that prides itself on being
so very mexicano.
Your presence adorns it
and your laughter is a bell
of enchanting ringing.
Here they are, beautiful lady
with a charming attitude,
horsemen on their steeds.
In every charro there's a man,
his boldness not to amaze you
whose gracefulness accompanies him. . . .
You will see him, sovereign one,
this beautiful morning
in the art of the charro. . . .
He will come to do flourishes at your feet
and once again in my poems
he will send his heart
to the foot of your altars.

When the summer ended at last, the songbirds flew
south, but the child had to fly north. He awaited the arrival
of Don Domingo Morales and the horse and wagon
beneath the dappled shade of an enormous spreading wild
fig, his duffel bag resting in the dirt. He was whiling away
the minutes playing rancho, which he had learned under
the tutelage of his summer companion. "See," the fair-
haired child had instructed, "with the small stones we will
make the corrales, and with the large stones the stables. The
large cow bones will be the bulls, the medium ones the
cows, the small ones the calves. The ribs will be the haci-

enda and the chapel, the sticks, the charros fighting the Porfiristas."

Francisco was distracted, nostalgic. He was thinking about how sad it would be to wrench himself, now deeply planted, out of the Mexican soil. Unexpectedly, there was a sound of jingling spurs and bridle, and a snorting and pawing on the ground. He looked up, first startled, then frightened by the looming vision before him: a tall, broad man on a well-bred horse, a palomino sixteen hands high. The man's eyes were squinting blue chips, his sideburns flecked with gray, his face tanned like the color of the tack hanging in the abandoned stables. His broad woven sombrero was encircled by an intricately woven band. His short jacket and chaps of fine leather were embroidered with rich threads. His botas were embossed black leather, the finely tooled saddle studded with silver, the rowels of his spurs sterling, his holstered pistols pearl-handled.

The boy was frightened, but polite. He sprang to his feet, trembling in the shadow of the great man and horse.

The man asked gruffly, "¿Cómo te llamas, hijo?"

"Francisco Valadéz, señor," he replied timidly, respectfully.

"Are you the son of Bentura Villalpando de Valadéz?" the charro queried, his voice now tender.

"Sí, señor," answered the boy, wondering.

"Then tell your mother that Don Javier Ortíz sends his regards and his love."

Then Don Javier reined his steed away abruptly, silently, and galloped toward the eastern horizon, his enormous dark shadow blocking out the sun and pinning Venus, the evening star, the love star, to his shoulder.

Amor Sufrido :: Long-Suffering Love

NO ME QUIERAS TANTO

Rafael Hernández

Yo siento en el alma tener que decirte
Que mi amor se extingue como una pabeza
Y poquito a poco se queda sin luz.
Yo sé que te mueres cual pálido cirio
Y sé que me quieres, que soy tu delirio
Y en esta vida, he sido tu cruz.
Ay amor, ya no me quieras tanto,
Ay amor, no sufras más por mi.
Si nomás puedo causarte llanto
Ay amor, olvídate de mi.
Me da pena que sigas sufriendo tu amor desesperado
Yo quisiera que tú encontraras de nuevo otro querer
Otro ser que te brinde la dicha
Que yo no te he brindado
Y poder alejarme de tí
Para nunca más volver.
Ay amor, ya no quieras tanto.
(Repeat)

Amor Sufrido :: Long-Suffering Love

Sunday, October 14, 1934
6 P.M.
Anselmo Vásquez
General Delivery
Kelsey, California

Miss Aurelia Celaya
Box 443
Jerome, Arizona

Dearest Honey Girl,
     Ay, gosh honey Prieta, but I'm tired tonight.
     I just had supper, and what a supper! I'm tired, Hon,
but happy in a way—and blue at the same time—being so
far from you, but in my heart, Prieta, you are always with
me.

We arrived here Friday night, all tired out from four hard days of driving. We rested yesterday and started to work today, Sunday, and how I worked! It's a gold mine, Honey, about ten miles from Placerville—way up in the Sierra Nevada—but oh, what beautiful country, Hon. I'm sure you will like it. I'm sure that this job is steady—at least I'm sticking, Hon. I've got to, Prieta—then we can eventually realize our plans.

I know I'll be able to save some nickels now. It's a long way to town, so there's no place to go. I wouldn't go anyhow—my mind is set.

I won't be able to batch for a while, Hon, as I would like to, as the company wants all single men to stay on the property and live at their bunkhouses and board at their mess hall. That's $1.00 a day I have to pay, but I believe I can come out okay. As soon as I can, I'll batch—that is, Paul and I. It will be a little harder, but it's well worth it to me.

Hon, I hope that all has been well with you and that not a dark cloud will mar the happy face I last saw—my smiling Pecosa. Gee, Hon, how I long to see you.

Remember that in the last fifteen months there were about seven days that I failed to see you. Little wonder that I'm lonely now. How I wish now I had always been good to you—if only half as good as you are to me. But Hon, I hope to God that someday I will be able to make up for everything. May I hope?

Well, Hon, answer soon, real soon, and make it long and sweet, as only you can write. I wish I could make my letters long and interesting like you, Hon, but I'm such a poor hand at it—terrible, don't you think?

I will close with worlds of love.
Your Hüero

There were always things that went BUMP IN THE NIGHT at our house—más o menos every other payday weekend on Friday or Saturday night: the fat rubbery sound of the car's front bumper against the carport wall (his depth perception was off). The tentative crunch of his shoes on the gravel driveway. The muffled creaking of the warped floor boards on the front porch (he had removed his cordovan shoes). The delicate tap-tap-tap-tap on the door frame (Mamá had locked the screen). The slow metallic turning of the skeleton key in the lock. The rusty creak of the front door hinges as it opened and closed (he'd remind himself to oil them with WD-40 tomorrow). The damp rush of Mamá's tears. The slurred excuses and mumbled apologies. The promises. The absolution. The quiet rhythmic creaking of their matrimonial bedsprings. And finally, the resonating snore of the deep sleep of a malcreant who knew he had been forgiven. Again.

I can tell you all this because our walls could talk, yes they really could. And they didn't just talk, believe me. They shouted. They whispered. They laughed and they cried. And, boy, could they ever sing—and it was always the same songs—like one of those lovesick ballads that Jacinto Orozco would play over and over again on KTUC Radio on La Hora Mexicana, until Death Do Us Part, Amen.

I could always tell what was coming even before it happened. I had radar, man. And eyes and ears just like Superman except I couldn't fly, but I wish I could have and

I would have flown out of there. I could see and hear though—it was like some bedtime story except this one kept me awake instead of letting me sleep: the padded shush, shush, shush of Mamá's slippers as she paced the linoleum floors. The hollow sucking sound of the icebox door opening and closing. The click of the burner on the gas stove so she could heat the cup of milk that would help calm her nerves and help her think straight. The sizzle of the lighted match for her cigarette. The sorrowful telegraph of her nails on the kitchen table ticking off the minutes past midnight like a clock. The papery swoosh, swoosh of the pages of the ladies' magazines she'd leaf through, unseeing, to pass the time until he came home (Gracias a Dios) safe, if not entirely sound. . . .

To tell you the truth, it didn't end up so bad. Life was pretty normal the intervening days between paychecks. Papá behaved pretty good—going to mass on Sunday morning, coming home from work early even. Bringing Mamá little presents like Camay Bath Talc in a tin from Jarrold's Drug Store or a box of chocolate-covered cherries or a soon-to-wilt chrysanthemum from the grocery store.

Oh, I tell you, Mamá was a real psychologist, she really was, and that's how they ended up staying together all those years. I thought she should get a job like one of those two big-haired sisters with the newspaper columns that you write to when you want to save your marriage. That's how good she was at figuring out things, and I told her so.

Anyway, this is the way it would go: There's Mamá, the morning after, in the kitchen, all fresh and crisp looking in her starched and laundered house dress, her curly ebony hair tied back from her face with a red grosgrain ribbon. His favorite color. And she smells like soap and bath powder. No makeup, just a hint of lipstick. She didn't need it. That's how beautiful she was. She's singing one of those romantic tunes that I told you about, along with the radio. "Solamente Una Vez" or "Anillo de Compromiso." Something like that. She's fixing a breakfast tray with hot coffee with sugar and cream ("Strong and dark, just like I like my women," he'd tease her) and buttered toast with homemade fig jam. Her steps are light and fast. Like dancing. I ask, "Mamá, what are you doing?" She looks up, startled to hear my bleary morning voice. I say, "You know Papá came home late last night after drinking and flirting at Manny's. Why are you spoiling him by taking him his coffee to bed?" She looks surprised, honest she does, suddenly aware that I've kept a vigil. She answers. She's SERIOUS. "Oh, m'hijita, I'm not spoiling him. I'm teaching him a lesson. He'll regret it, you'll see. When he finds out that I didn't stir the sugar in his coffee." And then she waltzes out the front door to get the morning newspaper and she folds it open to the sports section and places it lovingly on the tray, just like he likes it.

Some payday weekends, he'd slip a little more than others—like the time he left the car in Manny's parking lot and walked the six blocks home and then forgot about it. And when he woke up on Saturday morning he thought our car had been stolen and he called the police and there was all this upset and commotion and spying neighbors when the squad car was parked out in front of our house. And you can imagine Mamá's embarrassment when the police officer eventually found our station wagon parked exactly where Papá had left it.

It was times like this that the delicate truce would last through the weekend and sometimes into the middle of the week. And when things got that serious, no sweat, Mamá could always rely on what I liked to call her WASH DAY REVENGE; I'd know that negotiations were at a standstill when I'd come home from school after practicing for a procession (Sister Prudencia always had us practicing for one kind of procession or another, hoping, much to her eventual disillusionment, that if she kept us physically in line, the mental and the spiritual would follow). And I would see Mamá's "delicates" hanging on the clothesline in the backyard as far away from Papá's chonies as possible. "Atta girl, Mamá," I'd smile to myself. "You've got him where you want him now."

Then I'd go in through the back door and there would be, just as I had expected, dozens of our starched and perfectly ironed dresses hanging from every conceivable hook and curtain rod and from the tops of every door, like so many disembodied avenging angels. And she'd still be at it, her head lowered, her forehead beaded with perspiration in the stuffy kitchen, guiding that heavy old steam iron carefully—smoothing out the fabric of her life, ironing out the problems and inconsistencies, pressing out the crumpled dreams and puckered hopes. Until at last, those very same angels would carry her out of the now opened kitchen window—sailing, sailing, sailing away in the air with Mamá hanging by the most delicate of threads, until she arrived at that secret sanctuary of her soul where she could find another golden coin of trust and tuck it into the velvet bag of her heart and start all over again.

Amor de Madre :: Mother's Love

AMOR DE MADRE

Jesus Ramos

Dame por Dios
Tu bendición
O Madre mia adorada
Que yo a tus pies
Pido perdón
Por lo que tanto que has sufrido.
A donde estás en la mansión
Una mirada te pido
Madre querida
Ruega por mi al Creador
Tú que estás en la mansión
De ese reino celestial
Mándale a mi corazón
Un suspiro maternal,
Un suspiro maternal,
Un suspiro maternal,
Que me hiere, que me hiere el corazón.
Mira, Madre, que en el mundo
Nadie te ama como yo.
Mira que el amor de madre
Es tan grande como Dios
Mira, Madre, que en el mundo,
Nadie te ama como yo.
Se acabó el amor de madre
Que era mi única ilusión.

Amor de Madre :: Mother's Love

September 27, 1950
Seoul, Korea

Querida Madre:

The unusual happened today. I am spending my second day in the same foxhole. We are dug in on a hill southeast of Seoul. Sorry for not having written sooner, but so many things have happened since the Inchon landing on September 15th, that I haven't even had a chance to gather my thoughts.

It seems like I have lived twenty years of my life in these twelve days. It's been one difficult situation after another. As you know, the Tucson Company was split up back in Camp Pendleton, but we do run into each other as our paths cross. Although dying is very much a part of war, I still haven't gotten used to seeing it happen, especially when it's someone I know.

By now you've probably heard through Mrs. Estel Hubbard's Korean War Mother's Club that four of Tucson's "E" Company members have been killed. They were Corbett Robertson, Raymond Hubbard, Emilio Ramírez, and Jesús Carrasco. More of our members have been wounded. Thanks to your prayers, I have been spared. Poor Mrs. Hubbard. She went through all the trouble of organizing the families so that you could share the letters we send, and then her son is one of the first to get killed.

We fought all the way to Seoul, along the highway. The closer we got, the stiffer the enemy defense. I started out as the first ammo carrier for our machine guns squad, and on the fourth day our gunner was killed and our assistant gunner was badly wounded, so I became the new gunner.

We took Yong Dung Po with heavy losses. Then we crossed the Han River on amtracks, and the next day fought our way, block by block, through Seoul.

You know what they say—"que los hombres no lloran." Well, I cried in Seoul, but not from fear. We were at a barricade about to attack the next block, which we could not see too well because of the smoke from the burning buildings. Through the haze we saw someone coming. I had the machine gun trained on the man and could have dropped him in one burst. My squad leader was trying to unsling his carbine and was shouting for me to shoot. Something told me not to! As the man got closer, we could tell he was a civilian holding a young child—a girl about five years old—in front of him by the elbows. Her right knee was blown away and her leg was dangling from the tendons and flesh that were left! I was overcome with horror and pity for the little girl. The tears just flowed from my eyes and down my cheeks. Thank God I didn't shoot!

Please pray that I bear well under the horrors of war and that I will be able to adjust well when I return. I will be praying, also, that God gives you the strength to see you through our separation and keep you in the best of health and free from harm.

I miss all my family, but I miss you most of all. Give everyone my love.

You receive the heart of a son who loves you dearly.

Besitos para Ud.

Su hijo, Ruben

La viuda Eloisa Contreras awoke with the first serenade of Don Carlos Vigil's gallo, which perched, head ablaze with the rising sun, on the wooden slats of the dilapidated fence between their adjoining yards. The rooster, a magnificent Rhode Island Red, sang his mañanitas every morning with the first rays of dawn, and Doña Eloisa thought to herself, as her eyes opened slowly and adjusted to the thin gray light in her tiny bedroom, of how she depended on that song: it brought order where there was confusion; predictability where there was uncertainty; a glimmer of joy where there was sorrow, and hope where there was the threat of despair.

The gallo's exuberant alabanza mañanera warmed her heart with a blanket of memories and enveloped her first waking moments like her mother's rebozo of fine wool, which she kept safe with aromatic herbs in the bottom of the old metal trunk at the foot of the bed. The gallo sang of the sweet time now past: of barrio gardens now gone fallow, of old loves now in endless sleep, of the singsong backyard chatter of comadres now silenced by fear, of the joyful shouts of niños playing in the alleyways and dusty lanes— the same hijos now gone to fight a war and shouting from the mountaintops of a faraway land—a land whose name trilled on the Spanish tongue like a word in a sorrowful lullaby—Korea-Korea-Korea.

Doña Eloisa crossed herself and thanked Tata Dios and his army of saints for the gift of another day. Another Friday. And the breath to make another pilgrimage to la Misión de San Xavier in order to fulfill her manda—her promise—to pray on her knees on the hill of La Virgen for her son, and for all the sons of the barrio, that they might return safely from the war.

Doña Eloisa swung her slim but muscular legs over the edge of her single bed and felt with her feet for her chanclas, placed primly side by side on the faded hooked rug beside her bed. She stood slowly, stretching her arthritic joints that had stiffened overnight on the thin mattress, and shuffled to the small bathroom adjoining her bedroom. She went through the rituals of her morning ablutions methodically, lost in thought: a quick bath in tepid water; a splash of rose glycerine water on the delicate skin of her face, arms, and neck; a twist of her graying hair into a thick knot at the base of her neck; a liberal dusting of Camay powder. She dressed quickly then—thick cotton stockings, sturdy black shoes, and a long tunic of coarse brown manta cloth, which she tied loosely at the waist with a thick white cord and from which she suspended a well-worn rosary of black wooden beads.

Thus attired, she went into her kitchen, where the rays of the sun now radiated through the window that looked out onto her small garden. Like the fingers of God, she mused. She quickened her pace now—the sun was over the edge of the eastern horizon and would climb its great arch quickly in the late spring sky. She boiled water for her cup of Nescafé and her avena. The steaming bowl of oatmeal laced with melting butter and brown sugar, and pan de huevo dipped in her coffee sweetened with condensed milk would fortify her for her journey. She kept time by her vigil with the climbing sun—she must leave before seven o'clock, for the ten-mile trek, even at a steady pace, would take her five hours.

After eating breakfast, she packed a net bag with a simple lunch—a burro of refried beans and one of potatoes and egg that she had assembled the night before, a paper bag with some dried figs she had harvested from Don Carlos's higuera the previous summer, and a small bottle of water. She then gathered the two small cushions propped up on the sofa in the sala and tucked them into the bag. Finally, before her departure, she blew out the flame on the candle that burned on her living room shrine dedicated to El Santo Niño de Atocha—the patron of pilgrims and wanderers and prisoners. She recalled the words of Father Rossetti at the all-night prayer vigil held at the cathedral a fortnight ago: that the candles that burned out were a symbol of the complete sacrifice sometimes demanded of the soldiers who gave their lives for their country. She shivered in remembrance and touched lovingly the photograph of her son, resplendent in his Marine uniform, that stood alongside the bulto on her home altar. He was her only son, her youngest, only seventeen, but the reality of war had brought the flinty edge of manhood into the eyes of a boy overnight.

Doña Eloisa left by the back door of the kitchen and walked through a path in her small yard, which itself was beginning to recover from some frosty desert nights: there were buds on the lemon tree and the piocha, and tiny leaves sprouted greenly on the quince and rose bushes, and on the herbs in the tiny garden plot she had planted by her kitchen window. She swung open the gate made from an old iron bedstead. The gallo was long gone, giving his attention to more-mundane matters after the epiphany of the morning. Doña Eloisa turned right at the alleyway that flanked her house, then left on Ontario. The neighborhood's street was already stirring with early morning life: children frolicking on the way to El Río School, their homework and lunch boxes clasped in chubby hands; housewives in housecoats watering their flower beds and winter-browned patches of Bermuda grass; husbands backing their vintage cars carefully out of driveways on their way to work; abuelitos settling in comfortably with compadres on porch benches to reminisce about the Great War and light up their first cigarette of the day.

Doña Eloisa turned south upon reaching Grande Avenue. The street was paved and already bustling with activity and commerce. Father Estanislao, in the parking lot of Santa Margarita Church, was herding a group of excited schoolchildren into a dilapidated school bus for a field trip. Rafael Romero was pulling up the awning on the front window of his barber shop. "¿Cómo amaneciste, Doña Eloisa?" he called out in greeting. Francisco Ronquillo was setting out small tables in front of his panadería, and the aromas of his sweet breads and cookies, which he had been baking since 4 A.M., wafted in the morning air like the scents of an exotic garden. Gustavo Palafóx was cleaning the windows of El Grande Market, his cherubic face rosy with his efforts. Don Casimiro Moreno was raising the flags of México and the Estados Unidos at the Porfirio Díaz Mutualista Hall, struggling all the while with his one arm, for he had left the other on the beaches of Normandy. They all knew of her manda. And they greeted her with solemnity and with reverence: they bowed in respect, they smiled in greeting, they raised their hands in wordless blessings. And those very same blessings enveloped her like a protective mantle for her long trek of devotion: no inclement weather had befallen her, no stranger had been rude, no danger had loomed.

Doña Eloisa's well-clad feet marched resolutely toward her destination some ten miles south. They moved surely, automatically, and in her prayerful reverie she saw along the dusty shoulder of the road where she had walked, these long months of devotion, the depressions worn by her feet, weighed down by her heavy heart.

> Caminando, caminando, para aquella luz,
> En el aquel lugar donde está Jesús.

Grande merged with Mission Road, which twisted past the bruised flanks of Sentinel Hill and the old Warner Mill. Past the tiny adobe houses scattered like dominoes along the road. Caminando, caminando. Past the mesquitales that yearned from the banks of the Santa Cruz River—a river that flowed no more, but where today a silver ribbon of water from an unseasonable storm earlier in the week slowly turned to gold as the earth spun around the sun in a lambent sky. Caminando, caminando. Past the landfill at the San Cosme Convento site where Tucson's Hispanic history slumbered beneath the heaps of trash. Past the swimming hole at Silverlake where she imagined that she could still hear the horseplay of buquis as brown as coffee swinging from the protective muscular arms of the álamos. In time she could see on the eastern horizon the newly plowed fields of the Midvale Farms where the loamy black earth of the floodplain awaited warm nights for their green resurrection. Caminando, caminando. Mission Road merged onto the Papago Reservation. Doña Eloisa continued determinedly, never altering her pace. Past the huddled adobe houses where the late morning breakfast fires of fragrant mesquite sent their sweet incense heavenward to bless the day. Past the ancient windswept graveyard of the mission with its eroded mounds and tilting crosses of peeling paint and rusty iron, where her own ancestors from El Rancho de Los Reales slept side by side with their desert brethren.

> Caminando, caminando, para aquella luz,
> En el aquel lugar donde está Jesús.

A few more strides. Then, at last, Doña Eloisa raised her eyes to the great white towers of the centuries-old mission church standing like a stranded ark run aground on the desert's river plain. The milling tourists, expensive cameras slung around their necks, were dressed in the bright hues of tropical birds in the mating season. They stared at the humble brown figure dressed in her hábito as she approached the mission's massive wooden doors. She crossed the threshold, looking like a miniature figure in a diorama in contrast to the soaring nave of the church. She entered the cool darkness and made her way down the long aisle toward the carved and gilded main altar, which was shimmering like her companion, the sun, in the reflected light of a thousand flames of the faithful and the hopeful and the curious. When she arrived at the main altar, she bowed low, paying her respects to the Santísimo, all the while shutting out the drone of the chattering turistas protestantes. She bowed again, and then walked slowly to the western transept where the recumbent statue of San Francisco lay, as if asleep, in a carved wooden case. With wordless prayers, she kissed the forehead of the saint and then pinned a small metal milagro of a pierced heart on the blessed figure's satin coverlet. Thus spiritually refreshed, she went out once more into the brightness of midday. The ritual of her main devotion had yet to begin.

Doña Eloisa walked past the aromatic food stands of the Papago Indians who were selling frybread and red chile burros and roasted corn. A hundred yards to the east of the humming activity of the mission's plaza and parking lot was a small hill; a lonely figure, and alone, she laboriously climbed the rock-strewn narrow road of the volcanic plug, and when she reached the path to the summit, she sat in the scraggly shade of the only tree and ate her meager lunch and drank and rested. Then standing slowly, she removed from her lunch bag the two small cushions she had packed. She placed them strategically on the ground and then dropped to her knees carefully, resting each knee on a pillow. Then, inch by inch by inch, moving the pillows alternately with her knees, she navigated the path on the crest of the hill, which lay in the shadow of an enormous white wooden cross, and prayed out loud, in a barely audible whisper, the decades of the sorrowful mysteries of the rosary on the beads dangling from her waist. And when she arrived at last at her destination, the Virgin's Grotto, she stood painfully and gave thanks. Then she paused in heartfelt thought and scanned the horizon of the endless aquamarine sky. She had never seen the ocean, but nonetheless imagined that very sky above her to be the sea that lapped at this very moment on the shores of that faraway peninsula where the sons of the barrio lay bleeding and weeping. And then, when the updrafts of warm air from the afternoon sun sent the fair-weather cumulus scuttling in from the west, she imagined those clouds to be the great white ships that would carry the sons of the barrio home safely again.

Postscript

October 1998

Dear Patricia:

Thinking back on the letters written home from Korea—on my part, that is—things were very rarely informative, although at times I couldn't help but spill my guts. What was usually mentioned was how much I missed not seeing Mom and family and not being in Tucson. Mother's cooking was a biggy. We also wrote a lot about the end of the war.

On the comical side: Chino Munguía, who very much enjoyed partying, wrote to his mother and asked her to send him some money because now that he was heading for Korea to fight for his country, he needed to buy some ammunition for his rifle!

Raúl Reyes used to write weekly—one letter in Spanish to his mother where he left out anything that might worry her. Then to his sister he would write in English with more detailed information about what he was doing and about what was really going on. In one letter he mentioned being on a "mopping up" operation (i.e., having to hunt any enemy stragglers or rear guard). His sister had to translate the letter to his mother, and when she came to this part, his mother said, "Ay, qué bueno que tienen a mi hijo trabajando y trapeando en la cocina y no peleando!" Oh, how fortunate that they have my son working and mopping in the kitchen instead of fighting!

Few of the packages sent to Korea got to us, but on occasion, one or two got through. Niggie Romero remembers getting some green tamales once—not green corn tamales, but green with mold growing on them! The mold was scraped off, and the tamales were reheated and eaten. They were delicious! "Vice" Suárez remembers getting some tortillas in like condition. Once they were toasted, even the Anglos admitted liking these Mexican "crackers"!

I remember once writing to Mom and telling her how good a job her prayers were doing, but that it was all right to pray for a slight wound—something to get me off the battle line! Among my mother's papers, after she passed, I found a slip of paper with this prayer on it:

Con el velo del Santísimo Sacramento
Que sea mi hijo envuelto
Que no sea preso, herido ni muerto
Ni en manos del enemigo
El Padre lo cuide
El Espíritu lo salve
Dios con él siempre
Y contra él, Nada.

May the veil of the most holy Sacrament
Enfold and protect my son.
May he not be imprisoned or wounded or die
Nor fall into the hands of the enemy.
May the Father watch over him;
May the Holy Spirit redeem him,
May God be with him always;
May no obstacles ever lie in his path.

Good luck with your story,
Ruben Moreno

Amor Prohibido :: Forbidden Love

MINIFALDA

Lalo Guerrero

Ahora si se pelaron la barba
Con esa moda de las minifaldas
No dejan nada a la imaginación
Pués sí se agachan se les mira hasta la espalda
Tengo una nota que se llama Reynalda
También se pone ya su minifalda
Y cuando pasa, compadre del alma
Que hasta la lengua se escalda
Le canto así:
Reynalda, Reynalda,
Ay quítate tu minifalda
Que cuando bailas el go-go
Mira hasta la espalda
Reynalda, Reynalda,
Ya quítate tu minifalda
Que cuando bailas el go-go
Hasta la lengua se me escalda. . . .

Amor Prohibido :: Forbidden Love

Our cousin Lola would blow into town unexpectedly, like one of those summer dust devils that make you hang onto your hat for all it's worth and tuck your skirt between your legs. And like those impish and uncontrollable remolinos, she'd spin us toward her center with her energy and vitality. While Lola was visiting, rules and regulations, schedules and curfews were caught up in her willfulness and vivacity like confetti in a windstorm. . . .

Her arrival was always preceded by a letter written in the formal hand of our Tía Magdalena.

August 5, 1956
1492 W. 20th St.
Los Angeles, California

My dearest sister Yolanda:

I hope that this letter finds you and Raúl and the children happy and in the best of health. We are all well, gracias a Dios. Federico's back is much improved, and he has resumed driving the delivery truck. All the children—with one notable exception—are doing well in their studies and helping with various chores in our grocery store this summer.

Querida hermana, I am writing to you to ask you and Raúl a favor of the greatest import. Our eldest, your godchild Dolores, is causing us a great deal of grief this summer.

As you know, she is very much a señorita now, and although she is only fifteen, she is demanding the privileges of one much older. Our differences of opinion are causing a great deal of disruption in the family, and we are beside ourselves with worry. Why, only the other day my comadre Petra thought she saw her riding in a car with a pachuco on Hollywood Boulevard!

We are well aware of her high esteem and respect for you and Raúl since you are her godparents, and we are hopeful that a visit with you for the remaining two weeks of summer vacation might help settle her down and bring her to her senses.

I pray that this request prove to be not too great a burden and imposition. Please inform us of your decision as soon as possible. If you both agree to this arrangement, we

will buy her a ticket to Tucson on the next Greyhound bus.
Con mucho cariño y gratitud,
Tu hermana Magda

Our kindly and somewhat innocent mother (over our
father's protests—she already had enough to keep her busy
what with three children and cooking and cleaning and
sewing our clothes for the new school year; besides, my
sister and I were at a very impressionable age and Lola
might have a bad influence on our prepubescent minds)
phoned our Tía Magda immediately and said that she'd love
to have Lola come for a visit. We squealed with delight and
anticipation—having heard through the bedroom walls the
whispered discussions and disagreements about her deportment. Suddenly the prospect of the repetitious and tedious
summer routines of baby-sitting the Cocío brats, playing
Monopoly and Kick the Can and embroidering dishtowels,
dissipated like the heat in a chubasco.

We insisted on accompanying Mother and Father to the
dingy Greyhound bus station downtown. We waited in the
smoke-filled, old-clothes-smelling lobby for what seemed an
interminable amount of time—the bus was late as usual,
the air conditioner having broken down between Indio and
Yuma on schedule. When the silver leviathan pulled into its
parking slot at last, the door wheezed open and spilled a
passel of grumpy, rumpled, and bleary-eyed passengers. We
waited.

We heard Lola before we saw her—the high-pitched
laugh; the jangle of silver-plated bracelets on each arm; the
metallic clink of the taps on her platform shoes; the snap

and crack of her Juicy Fruit gum. Then she appeared at long last—framed in the doorway of the bus—our prima Lola, resplendent in a teased blonde (!) pompadour; magenta, heart-shaped mouth setting off perfect white teeth; false eyelashes fringing dark eyes smudged with green eye shadow; glimmery dress showing off her youthful curves to advantage.

A long, low appreciative whistle echoed from somewhere in the portico. "¡Quéhubole!" she shouted over the din of the diesels. "How are my cute little cousins doing?" She cast an incredulous and critical glance at our modest homemade cotton frocks with the Peter Pan collars and puffed sleeves. Then she hugged us enthusiastically, and we swooned in the fragrance of her drugstore cologne. The ride home, which must have seemed interminable to our father, was noisy, the din trapped by the closed windows of the car—Lola talking too loud, and us squealing in appreciation at her exaggerated tales of the trip.

Our prima, Lola! A California Home Girl! A teenager! Knowledgeable. Daring. Streetwise. The keeper of the keys to the kingdom of romance: boys and cars, flirting and dating, drive-in movies, lovers' lanes, making out and French kissing, and the sensual sandy beaches of the California paradise we could only fantasize about.

She shared our small bedroom with us, sleeping on the double bed while my sister and I took turns on the rollaway. Our tiny room was transformed into a garden of earthly delights when the contents of her suitcase—cosmetics, jewelry, accessories, dresses, and shoes in shimmering hues—spilled out onto every available surface of the bed, the bureau, the floor, and the lone chair. We'd whisper and

giggle far into the night after our tolerant mother had
tucked us in ("Now I lay me down to sleep. I pray the Lord
my soul to keep. If I should die before I wake, I pray the
Lord my soul to take, God Bless Mommy and Daddy and
Cousin Lola and make us good little girls, Amen"). She
entertained us with the stories of her escapades—many, I
think now in retrospect, embellished for her appreciative
audience. We increased and improved our vocabulary in
Spanish. We thought our mother would be pleased. Ya
chole, ya estufas, waifa, aruca, carcancha, chota, a toda
madre, andar pimpo, buey, hay te wacho, carnal. "Fuimos
con la clica a un piquiniqui en la carcancha de Chuy. No
escuadras allowed. Anduvimos a todo pimpo. Tuvimos un
good time a toda madre." (We went with our clique in
Chuy's car to a picnic. No squares allowed. We were all
dressed up and had a great time!)

But the highlights of Lola's visits were our occasional
trips to the McClellan's Five and Dime on Congress Street
downtown. Lola always feigned helpfulness. "Would you
like me to take the girls to the library, Tía? On the way
home we can stop at the dime store if you need us to run an
errand. Do you need thread, elastic, buttons, shampoo,
dishtowels, bath powder, hairpins?" Our frazzled mother,
eager for a break, and delighted in our pursuit of and
sudden interest in the summer reading program, would
send us off with a list and her blessing. We'd catch the bus
on Grant and Stone, disembark at the corner of Stone and
Congress, and then walk the two blocks to McClellan's on
the corner of Scott. There, after purchasing the few necessi-
ties with which our mother had entrusted us, we'd cruise
the aisles of the store (under the ever vigilant eyes of the

salesclerks, who by the summer's end were bored and tired of policing adolescent girls) with Lola as our tour guide.

We'd leaf through the steamy magazines (*True Romance, True Detective, Modern Love*) with their photographs of blue-eyed, light-skinned beautiful people intertwined in amorous poses. We'd amble down to the "Intimates" counter and giggle over D-cup bras, girdles, falsies, lacy undies, and black and red lingerie. We'd check out the fragrance section and anoint ourselves liberally with cheap perfumes from tester bottles labeled "Forbidden," "Passion," "Danger," and "Temptation." Our final destination was always the cosmetics counter, where we'd transform ourselves with sampler tubes of lipstick ("Fire and Ice," "Cherries in the Snow," "Raspberry Embrace") and a whole palette of eye shadow, eye liner, and rouge, with our prima all the while tutoring us with a running commentary of the benefits of tweezers, razors, depilatories, face creams, astringents, breath fresheners, body powder, deodorants, nail polish, hair coloring, and skin whiteners.

We'd watch the clock and then rush to our obligatory visit to the Andrew Carnegie Library on South Sixth Avenue (with its marble bench of the scantily clad and suggestively posed goddesses at the entrance) where we'd check out our usual summer selections of the *Adventures of Nancy Drew* and *The Hardy Boys*. (The kindly librarian, Miss Maxwell—who knew about our mother's lofty literary goals for us—must have been startled by our clumsy and failed attempts at glamour, but she kept her counsel and only smiled thinly at us with arched eyebrows.) Then we'd sashay down Congress to T. Ed Litt's Drugstore for a coke at the soda fountain and a quick trip to the Ladies' Room to remove any telltale traces of our "makeovers" before catching the 4:00 bus that, like Cinderella's pumpkin coach, would transport us back into the fold of our ordinary and predictable world.

Thus the two weeks flew by, and before we knew it, it was time (too soon!) for our cousin Lola to be returned to her long-suffering parents. We drove with her to the bus station in silence and melancholy. To our dismay, the bus departed on time. She boarded with her usual flourish and waved good-bye (¡Hay te wacho!) through the gray film of the bus window. We waved disconsolately in turn. The bus gave a great sputtering belch of diesel fumes, pulled out of the station, and rolled onto Congress Street. We watched it until it became a small dot on the westward horizon, heading into the setting sun that would drop into the great watery blue world of Califas.

Our father was visibly relieved. "Well, I'm glad that's over. What an ordeal—the two weeks seemed like two months!"

"Now, Raúl, dear," Mother interjected expansively. "Don't be too critical of Dolores. She's really a very sweet girl. She just has a good imagination. She's very artistic and dramatic, that's all. Why, she'll probably end up being a clothing designer or actress or writer, or something. And besides, you should keep in mind that she's quite a role model and tutor for the girls because she's bilingual."

"Yes," I piped in brightly. "At least she's not an esquadra. She's quite a chamacona. Muy benota y entacuchuda." (She's not a square. She's quite a gal and a sharp dresser, too.)

August 1, 1980
Riverside, California

My dearest Tío Raúl and Tía Yolanda:

I hope that this letter finds you both happy and in the best of health. We are all fine, thank goodness. The business in my beauty shop and boutique is going well: we are opening another store soon in San Bernardino. Luís is indispensable as my accountant and sales manager!

Dearest Ninos, I am writing to ask you both a favor of great import. Our eldest, Raquel, is causing us a great deal of grief this summer. She is sullen and lazy and given to talking back. All she wants to do is watch MTV and hang out in the mall with her friends. She says she will go on a hunger strike if we don't let her date. I am remembering my summer visits with you with much fondness and was wondering if Raquel might come and spend a week or so with you before school begins. I know such a visit would have a positive influence on her—I remember especially our inspiring visits to the library. Please let me know if my request is not too much of an imposition. If you agree to the visit, I will send her to Tucson on the very next plane.

With much love,
    your niece Dolores

Amor Desesperado :: Desperate Love

SIN UN AMOR

Alfredo Gil and Chucho Navarro

Sin un amor
La vida no se llama vida
Sin un amor
Le falta fuerza el corazón
Sin un amor
El alma muere derrotada
Desesperada en el dolor
Sacrificada sin razón
Sin un amor no hay salvación. . . .

Amor Desesperado :: Desperate Love

The following note was confiscated by Sister Prudencia in May 1964 from Anna Ortiz as she was passing it to her best friend, Martita López, in English class, Period 4, at Salpointe Catholic High School in Tucson, Arizona. The note remains on file in her records along with a copy of Anna's report card; the following infractions in deportment are highlighted in red pencil: Is Inattentive; Wastes Time; Annoys Others. The end result of this ill-timed discovery causing her to be grounded for a whole month, not that she had been invited to the prom anyway. . . .

Dear Martita,
   Wow! What a sexy English composition class this is with Sister Pee Wee droning on and on about dangling

participles and ejaculations!!!! Ha. Ha. Geez, I feel hysterical, panicked, depressed, and desperate. The Junior-Senior Prom is only two weeks away and I don't have a date, but my sister does, natch, and my mom made her a taffeta dress that took four yards just for the skirt. Maybe I could go stag—just kidding. Did I tell you about the joke I made up? Do you know why they call them nuns? Because they don't get any. ("Nones"—Get it?) Ha. Ha. Whoops, better sign off. I see Pee Wee is eyeing me. Burn this.

Anna

P.S. Have you voted for my sister for prom queen yet? You better!

Part 1: The Rules

Don't wear your hair too long or you'll look like a pachuca, or too short or you will appear mannish. Keep your ankles crossed, your toes pointed, your knees together, your chin up, your head high, your eyes down (but not shifty), your back erect, your shoulders straight. If you are too quiet, he'll think you are moody; too talkative, frivolous. Too thin, sickly; too plump, lazy. Too studious, haughty; unlearned, dull. Too active, restless; too placid, morose. Too generous, careless; too thrifty, selfish. Too devout, prudish; faithless, loose. If you eat too much, he'll consider you a glutton; not enough, finicky. And try to remember to keep your hands elevated vertically whenever possible so that the veins don't pop out. And never never never go out of the house without a fresh set of underwear that is in good condition because you never know if you'll be in an accident.

Part 2: The Recipes

FOR THE HAIR

My abuelita's secret tonic for lustrous hair that will be
sure to catch his eye is as follows:
6 ounces ethyl rubbing alcohol or strong proof vodka
1 ounce nettle
1 ounce rosemary
12 drops castor oil
1 ounce salycilic acid
1 ounce distilled water
Directions: Soak the nettle and the rosemary in the
alcohol for a week. Strain into another container and add
castor oil and perfumed herbs. Dissolve salycilic acid in
distilled water and add to herbal and oil solution and use as
a rinse on the hair.

Another tonic for the hair can be made by using gum
camphor: Steep 1 ounce of crushed gum camphor and two
ounces of powdered borax into two quarts of boiling water
for several hours. Massage nightly into the hair and then
brush for five hundred strokes. (At times it can be quite
helpful to sip the vodka from the first recipe while brushing
the hair.)

FOR THE COMPLEXION

A complexion cleansing and circulation mask is made
of the following:
¼ cake of camphor
1 egg white
1 peeled cucumber

¼ teaspoon lemon juice
1 teaspoon ethyl alcohol
1 teaspoon witch hazel
3 drops peppermint oil extract
Directions: Crush camphor; add to whipped egg white and cucumber. Blend together. Add lemon juice or cider vinegar, alcohol, witch hazel, and peppermint oil extract. Blend again. Apply as a mask and allow to dry while reclining with feet elevated in a darkened room. Remove in fifteen or twenty minutes. Rinse thoroughly. Close your pores with a strong astringent. (This may sting.)

For Body Odor

An antiperspirant drink that has a valued reputation is made of camphor, lemon, and milk. Soak the peeling of a lemon in warm milk and add three drops of camphor oil to the milk. Before sleeping, drink the milk and chew the rind.

For Fresh Breath

Camphor chalk has two virtues: one in being an inert substance, and the other in being an antiseptic. It is therefore valuable for dental purposes, keeping the teeth white and the breath fresh. Make a paste as follows:
1 teaspoon camphor
1 lump sugar
1 tablespoon crushed almonds
½ pint distilled water
Directions: Powder the camphor and the sugar. Grind

the almonds in a molcajete and make a paste by adding distilled water. Brush your teeth six times a day for at least ten minutes. (It is also helpful to brush the tongue.)

FOR THE HANDS

Lemon peel rubbed on fingernails strengthens and also cleanses and whitens. A wonderful nail restorer combines equal parts of honey, avocado, egg yolk, and a pinch of sea salt. Rub into nails. Leave for an hour and then rinse off. (This is also useful for whitening the skin, which is a very desirable attribute for getting a summer job.)

FOR THE FEET

Massaging the feet with olive oil will soften the dead tissue and make it easier to rid oneself of impediments. (Physical, not emotional.)

FOR THE EYES

A tea made of rose hips can reduce puffiness under the eyes. Make a paste of rose hip powder and small additions of parsley, cucumber, lemon peel, and sliced strawberries. Pat on the eyes and allow to dry, preferably with the head at a 45 degree angle. Remove after one hour with warm water.

[In addition, a tea made from the flower of the elderberry tree is an excellent remedy for twitching eyelids, but I can't remember if my abuelita told me to drink it, daub it on my eyelids, or bathe in it. Perhaps all three, if the condition is serious enough.]

For All Disorders of the Body

Garlic has many medicinal uses, including controlling worms, treating scorpion bites, colds, hoarseness, indigestion, and asthma. One old curandera who was a neighbor of my abuelita in Barrio Hollywood describes the use of the center bulbet: Insert into the left ear to relieve symptoms of nervousness.

A cup of tea made from sage, dandelion flowers, and honey will help to bring on a sense of calmness. In addition, hierba buena is an herb that grows wild in the garden. Peppermint tea makes an excellent tonic that strengthens and cleanses the entire body and is soothing to the nerves. (For a headache, drink some tea and lie down for a little while.)

[The aforementioned ingredients can serve multiple uses should one or more of the tonics or potions fail in their purported usefulness. In various stages of discouragement, I have been known to make smoothies, salads, mixed drinks, appetizers, and salad dressings as a last resort.]

Part 3: The Saints (When All Else Fails)

San Antonio, Evadio, Flavio, Bonifacio, Ubaldo, Venancio, Bernardino, Valente, Epitacio, Donascio, Urbano, Fernando, Marcelino, Norberto, José, Roberto, Gilardo, Feliciano, Cirilo, Bernabé, Nazario, Eliseo, Modesto, Silverio, Paulino, Juan Bautista, Anselmo, Cornelio, Camilo, Cayetano, Plutarco, Pedro y Pablo, Abundio, Isaias, Nabor, Arnulfo, Vicente, Joaquín, Celestino, Próspero, Justo, Emiliano, Acacio, Eusebio,

Librado, Sixto, Filiberto, Jacobo, Bartolomé, Luís Rey,
Armando, Agustín, Ramón, Judas, Efren, Carlos, Zacarías,
Leonardo, Ernesto, Victorino, Teodoro, Diego, Leopoldo,
Fidencio, Ponciano, Gelasio, Erasmo, Crisogno, Conrado,
Esteban, Saturnino, Andrés, Francisco, Ambrosio, Damaso,
Filogenio, Tomás, Demetrio, Patricio, Silvestre . . . and
Santa Imelda, Enedina, Prudencia, Rita, Carolina, Teodosia,
Petronilla, Elena, Clotilde, Emma, Socorro, Filomena,
Isabela, Amalia, María Magdalena, Brigida, Cristina,
Esperanza, Lidia, Paulina, Susana, Clara, Aurora, Beatríz,
Silviana, Aurelia, Cecilia, Natalia, Bárbara, Concepción,
Leocadia, Lucía, Victoria, Adelaida, Nuestra Señora de
Guadalupe, Nuestra Señora de Perpetuo Socorro, Virgen
del Carmen, Virgen de la Soledad, Virgen del Rosario,
Virgen de San Juan de Los Lagos, Sagrada Familia, Santo
Niño de Atocha, Santo Niño de Praga . . . *please* help me
find a husband that will meet my mother's high standards,
Amen.

Amor Encantado :: Enchanted Love

LA BRUJA (LA MACETA)

Alfredo Kayser

Ay, que bonito es volar
A las dos de la mañana
A las dos de la mañana
Ay que bonito es volar, ay mamá
Para venir a caer
En los brazos de su dama
En los brazos de su dama
Hasta queriendo llorar, ay mamá.
Me agarra la bruja,
Me lleva a su casa
Me vuelve maceta
Me da calabaza
Ay dígame, dígame, dígame Ud.
Cuantas criaturitas se ha chupado Ud.
Ninguna, ninguna, ninguna, no sé
Ando en pretenciones de chuparme a Ud.

Amor Encantado :: Enchanted Love

It was the high tourist season in the Old Pueblo de Tucson. The airport lobby was jammed with travelers and odd-shaped pieces of luggage carrying the required accessories for the Sunbelt pilgrims—golf clubs, tennis racquets, and cowboy boots and hats. The taxis and hotel shuttles and rental cars were backed up in the exit lanes of the toll booths all the way to the entrance kiosks. Everyone was headed north to the foothills' five-star resorts where spectacular mountain and sunset views were guaranteed. It was to be a season to end all seasons—the long-range forecast from the gray-haired, gray-faced, gray-jacketed weather announcer on the local news station promised balmy weather in the high 70°s, no rain, a gentle breeze, a waxing moon in a clear starlit sky, and the perfect alignment of planets—Venus in conjunction with Jupiter. All this, of course, was based on the failproof technology of computers, satellites, radar, and the science of meteorology; the weatherman himself was highly allergic to fresh air and made it his policy never to step outdoors unless it was to stroll to his car, which delivered him unpollinated to the air-conditioned comfort of the mall or his doorstep or the airport when it was his wont to take a vacation in the opposite direction of the arriving turistas.

All the señoras and señoritas on the household staffs of Ventana Canyon, La Paloma, El Conquistador, and the Westward Look hotels were working overtime in preparation for the arriving hordes—fluffing up pillows and towels, stocking mini-refrigerators, arranging fresh flowers and fruit, and spraying first-class rooms with aerosol scents of desert blooms. The señores and mozos, too, guapos in their Sonoran vaquero hats, were working sleeveless in the warm spring sun perfecting the ambience: skimming the surfaces of the swimming pools and fountains with delicate nets, blowing dried leaves and litter from the flagstone and tile walkways, trimming bushes and palm trees and tropical vines, clipping and mowing and taking care of the huge expanses of lawns, and planting annuals—pansies and petunias and snapdragons and delphiniums and larkspur— so that the peregrinos could enjoy the Southwest atmosphere without becoming too nostalgic for the temporarily abandoned flora of their hometowns.

The pools were heated, the rooms were cooled, the Coronas iced, the salsa tangy, the guacamole ambrosial. Perfection and predictability were the operative words: Nothing else would do for King and Queen Tourist in the Tucson Chamber of Commerce's Kingdom of Magic and Make-Believe.

But as the ancient dicho says in Spanish—"El hombre pone y Dios dispone"—a proverb also immortalized by the great Scottish bard—"The best-laid plans of mice and men gang aft agley"—which, in short, in any language, warns the over-confident not to make too many plans. For as luck or the stars or Tata Dios would have it, the high season of turismo in Tucson also coincided with the high season of the miraculous powder—los polvos milagrosos—in the barrios of south and central Tucson. And that very night sky that brought the planets and the stars and the moon into perfect alignment, and brought the hüeritos to swooning and romancing and making promises in the resort cantinas and balconies were the very same constellations that gave hope to all the old maids, bachelors, widows, widowers, the jilted, the lovelorn and the lonely and the less than desirable (and, I might add, their optimistic mothers) of el pueblo viejo. And anyone steeped in mexicano tradition, hearsay, rumor, magic, to say nothing of a smattering of theology, knew of the polvos milagrosos that Don Ramón Garcia sold off of revolving racks at the Tres Esquinas Farmacia and Hierbería on South Stone Avenue. The powders—which were sold for two dollars in one-ounce portions in miniature plastic bags (and smelled suspiciously like Johnson's baby talc)—if sprinkled in the right place at the right time, in the right season with the right intentions and the right prayers to the right saints, guaranteed romance and true love.

And business at the Tres Esquinas Farmacia had never been better—so good that the eager customers began waiting before the farmacia opened, clutching their coin purses and wallets while standing in a line that backed all the way to El Tecolote Fruit Stand on Twenty-ninth Street, where Don Heriberto Murillo, the enterprising proprietor, opened earlier than usual to wait on the anxious and bored, selling them a few cans of soft drinks, flour tortillas, cajeta and membrillo candy, and a few pounds and sprigs or bags of this and that.

Doña Pomposa was the first in line at the farmacia, after having attended the 6 A.M. Mass at Santa Cruz Catholic Church (just to make sure that all of her bases were covered). She waited stoically, arm in arm with her plain and nervous daughter Petronilla who, after having been left thrice at the altar, had developed a nervous tic in her right eye. Señora Refugia, with her bachelor son who had been mustered out of the seminary due to bad breath and a faltering intellect, was next in line, followed by Don Leonardo, who leaned on his cane and wheezed in the exhaust-laden air of the morning commuter traffic. An octogenarian, he was ever hopeful, having outlived three previous wives and having decided that he would request a twenty-something virgin who could make tortillas. The list of wishes was extensive and varied: Pious Rosario prayed for a platonic union; Señora Soto was there with her son because he was too short; Doña Brígida with her daughter because she was too tall; Aurora wished for a suitor with a red convertible; la viuda Celia, because she was lonely in the company of her six cats, wished for a compañero who could help her with the yard work; and the beautiful Margarita prayed for a caballero who could dance all the tandas at El Casino Ballroom without taking a break or perspiring.

The farmacia opened on the dot at seven o'clock, and Don Ramón, bearded and be-ringed like an oriental potentate, was perched, as expected, on a high stool in his mezzanine office, keeping a careful watch over the customers and the salesclerks. The Tres Esquinas Farmacia and Hierbería sold liniment, potions, prescription medicine, hierbas, soaps, cosmetics, candles, novelas románticas, plaster saints, and an odd assortment of curios from south of the border: armadillo purses, cholla cactus lamps, hand-tooled cowboy belts and wallets, pot hangers made from the cojones of bulls, and tarantulas and scorpions in amber. But by far the most popular item on this day of days were the aforementioned polvos milagrosos—each with the particular saint and pertinent instructions and prayers inserted into the plastic bag: legítimo polvo de San Ramón, legítimo polvo de Santa Clara, legítimo polvo de San Antonio, legítimo polvo de Santa Marta, legítimo polvo de San Judas para ganar una mujer o un hombre (for the most desperate of cases). The instructions: Put this powder in your right hand and blow it around your house—not forgetting the doorway, the windowsills, the hallways—while saying the prayer and thinking of your intended loved one. Recite this novena while sprinkling this powder on the sidewalks where the object of your desire might be walking. Pray this litany while powdering yourself. Sing these hymns while dispersing this polvo on the rooftop of your house, your gardens, the curbs, the alleyways, the driveways. Sprinkle this powder into the drink of your one and only while reciting this prayer to San Valentín:

Oh, my Saint, I am lonely.
Help me, great Saint, for
Thou knowest the mysteries
Of the human heart.
Grant me what I desire.

Grant me a good husband (wife)
Who will follow the law of true love.
So shall my love be. . . .
So shall my love be. . . .
Through thy powder,
Oh Blessed Valentine, Amen.

Etcetera, etcetera, etcetera . . .

Little did Doña Amalia realize that she would change
the course of local history and social demographics when
she stepped out onto her backyard stoop and startled a hen
who was having a dust bath under the rickety porch. The
gallina, terrified that her slothful ways had been discovered
and that she might be destined thus to be next in line for
the mole pot, with a loud squawking and an erratic flapping
of her wings ran to the protection of the henhouse where
she hurriedly sat on her nest and made earnest clucking
noises. But in keeping with the now well-known chaos
theory of quantum physics—if a butterfly flaps its wings in
Hawaii, it can cause a hurricane in the Virgin Islands,
etc.—that very same terrified and urgent flapping of Doña
Amalia's laying hen caused a shift, not only in the velocity,
but in the direction of the winds, and before the weatherman had time to change his forecast, the gentle breeze had
developed into gusts, which developed into a chubasco,
which developed into a gale that swirled all the polvos
legítimos of the lovesick from Barrio El Hoyo, Barrio Anita,
Barrio Hollywood, and Barrio Libre toward the general
direction of the foothills and neatly deposited them in
powdery sifting layers on the tiled rooftops and elegant

gardens and romantic balconies of all the aforementioned first-class tourist accommodations.

There was an immediate reaction of alarm when at first the polvos were thought to be snow. But when those in charge of tourist comforts realized it was but a powdery white dust, they kept the phones ringing off the hook at the Downtown Convention and Visitors Bureau with their complaints. The receptionists, the concierges, the golf and tennis pros, the executive chefs, the hotel managers, and even the hotel owners themselves from corporate headquarters in Los Angeles, demanded an explanation of the unseasonable haze that was contaminating the views.

But let it become part of the official record that the turistas themselves were unusually quiet about the matter, and the sunsets and sunrises in the polvo-laden atmosphere were incredibly breathtaking. And Michael, the architect from Wisconsin, snuggled with Juanita the chambermaid after having ordered room service and hanging a "Favor de No Molestar" sign on the door of his suite at La Paloma. And Francisco, the landscaper, having just arrived through a hole in the fence in Nogales and not knowing a word of English, much less Greek, strolled arm in arm with an exiled princess from the Aegean Islands down the torch-lit paths of the gardens of La Ventana. And Dr. Goldman, the balding heart surgeon from Beverly Hills, danced cheek to cheek with Carlota the waitress in the Hasta Mañana Lounge of the El Conquistador Hotel. And the blonde law clerk from the firm of Libby and Thomas and Miller, P.C., whispered sweet nothings into the ear of Rafael the wrangler over a candlelit dinner in the Gold Room of the Westward Look (she treated). And Enrique the busboy lounged poolside sipping Tequila Gold shooters with salt and lime out of silver thimbles with a widowed heiress from Boston. And all the crew from the Sabino Canyon Ranch and Spa—Paco and Flaco, Chino and Indio, Húilo and Gordo, Chulo and Feo, Huero and Prieto—took turns taking a spin in a rented Thunderbird convertible to see the city lights from the parking lot on Windy Point on the Mount Lemmon Highway with the feminist policy wonks of the National Organization for Women headquartered in Washington, D.C.

Amor Frustrado :: Frustrated Love

Amor Frustrado :: Frustrated Love

El Tiradito is a highly revered and sacred shrine on the corner of Main and Simpson in the Barrio Histórico of the Pueblo Viejo de Tucson where all the energy and power and spirits of love spells converge. And lest it be forgotten by posterity, let it be noted that the nicho itself was rescued by the power of love through the efforts of the Barrio Neighborhood Association when its destruction to make way for a highway interchange seemed imminent. It was through the involvement, finally, of Doña Leocadia—viuda de Ramírez, Zamora, Acuña, and Fimbres (who had found her four hapless husbands due to the miraculous intercession of The Little Fallen One)—that the earth-moving machines from the Department of Transportation, finding her prostrate in their paths, backed up and rumbled away never to return.

Indeed, it is at this very location, which is the site of a now dried-up spring, that a now famous assignation occurred between a mestiza washerwoman from Pitiquito and an investment banker from New York. But that is another story.

At any rate, the legend of El Tiradito and its many variations center around a young and presumably innocent vaquero from Los Reales named Juan Rulfo who was killed—mistakenly or deservedly—as a result of a love triangle which may or may not have been a case of mistaken identity, somewhat on the theme of being in the wrong place at the wrong time, which in this case was in the vicinity of a jealous husband who sought to avenge the honor of his fair but perhaps borderline virtuous wife. Alas, poor Juan Rulfo, before he had a chance to explain his presence in the boudoir of the beautiful Anastasia, ran for his life and was done away with unceremoniously on the very spot where the shrine is located—the speed of a silver bullet being faster than the speed of sound, especially unrehearsed explanations.

Juan was buried, 'tis believed, under the very tree where he fell (although his actual fall from grace has never been determined). And now for more than a hundred years his tomb has been a place of veneration where petitions and prayers for love are placed, challenging the imagination of the cynical who wonder why one so unlucky at love should be the intercessor for matters of the heart, but perhaps it can be supposed that he learned something in the process.

The Spells

The spell basics for El Tiradito are as follows:

His favorite colors: Pink to dark pink. Not red unless you just want sex.

Herbs and fragrances: Lavender, rosemary, orange, and lemon peel.

Flowers: Rose, jasmine, and violets. Gardenia if you want no sex.

Precious stones: Jade, pearls, and rubies.

Day to attract a man: Friday.

Day to attract a woman: Tuesday.

Time of the month: Between the new moon and the full moon.

Time of day: Third hour of darkness.

Instructions: Light a twenty-four-hour candle, and if it burns completely without being extinguished—even in the rain and strongest wind—then your wishes for a lover will come true.

Prayer:

O my martyred El Tiradito
Thou who sufferest and expirest for love
Grant that I may meet the man (woman) of my dreams
Who is handsome, hard working, and drives a nice car,
Amen.

P.S. Great caution must be exercised by those practicing

a devotion to El Tiradito. You must be forewarned to avoid the shrine during the hottest months of the summer. There is a well-known tale about a young maiden (whose name will remain anonymous) who lit her candle and prayed her novena at high noon on the twenty-fourth of June when all the townspeople were down on the banks of the Santa Cruz River bathing and praying for rain, it being the Fiesta de San Juan. Alas, much to her embarrassment and humiliation, she found herself mired in four feet of candle wax, the result of a century of supplications at the shrine. Due to the weekend partying, it was two days before she was rescued, and needless to say, her peau de soie slippers had been completely and irretrievably ruined.

Amor e Ilusión :: Love and Illusion

DE COLORES

De colores, de colores se visten los campos en la
primavera.
De colores, de colores son los pajaritos que
vienen de afuera.
De colores, de colores es el arco iris que vemos
lucir.
Y por eso los grandes amores de muchos colores
me gustan a mí.
Y por eso los grandes amores de muchos colores
me gustan a mí.

Canta el gallo, canta el gallo con el quiri, quiri,
quiri, quiri, quiri, qui.
La gallina, la gallina con el cara, cara, cara, cara,
cara.
Los polluelos, los polluelos con el pío, pío, pío,
pío, pí.
Y por eso los grandes amores de muchos colores
me gustan a mí.

Amor e Ilusión :: Love and Illusion

1 de agosto de 1989
Tucson, Arizona

Doña Amparo Bustamante, Vda. de Rodríguez
730 S. Mission Lane
Tucson, Arizona

Querida Comadre Amparito:

Te estoy escribiendo estas cuantas líneas para darte las gracias del fondo de mi corazón por haberme venido a ver la semana pasada en la hora de mi dolencia por la muerte de mi querido pariente, Don Tomás. Gracias por tu presencia en los ritos fúnebres, el rosario, y la misa del cuerpo presente. Agradezco mucho tus oraciones y novenas.

También te quiero dar las gracias por los antojitos sabrosísimos que me trajiste—sabes muy bien que con mi tristeza no tengo mucho apetito, pero siquiera me animé un poquito para probarlos. Además, te quiero dar las gracias por el tiempo que pasaste conmigo hablando de la vida ajena y espero que puedas visitarme muy en seguida porque tu presencia me anima—al pesar de las tristezas de la vida—para seguir viviendo con esperanza y con fe.

Con mucho cariño y gratitud, tu comadre,
Doña Altagracia Soto, Vda. de Morales

My dearest Comadre Amparito:

I am writing these few lines to thank you from the bottom of my heart for visiting me last week at my time of great sorrow. Thank you, also, for your presence at the funeral rites of my dearly departed relative, Don Tomás. Your prayers are very much appreciated.

Thank you, also, for the delicious food—how well you understand that with my sadness I have not felt much like eating, but your generosity boosted my appetite a tad. I look forward very much to your next visit. News of the outside world gives me reason—in spite of the tragedies of life—to continue living with hope and faith.

With much affection and gratitude,
Altagracia

Straight as an arrow flies (or la bala perdida, for that matter), Paco Miranda's misfired bullet (where he was hunting rabbits in the mesquital along the banks of the Santa Cruz River) whizzed west on Congress, made a left turn on Grande, another left on Melwood, and embedded itself in the caliche in a cottonwood-shaded corral in Barrio

San Cosme near the banks of the río. The bullet's arrival was timed with that of a dilapidated '57 Ford whose original forest green paint had faded to a hierba buena mint tone after decades of being parked in the relentless Arizona sun.

The rattling of the sedan, driven by Doña Amparo Rodríguez (an octogenarian who hadn't renewed her license in twenty years, but no matter, she only drove the car the three blocks from her casita on Mission Lane to her comadre's on her weekly visits), was a wake-up call to the dozens of dozing feathered, furry, and scaly creatures who were having a late-morning siesta in the yard. Cantínflas, the mongrel watchdog who was a genetic compilation of every breed ever registered with the AKC, was asleep belly up, patas arriba, under an ancient alamo. Roused, he gave chase to the napping tomcat, Plácido, who gave chase to a slumbering rooster under the nopal, who then gave chase to his pretty pullets, who then gave chase to the grasshoppers now clacking in the patches of Bermuda grass by the front porch of the small adobe home painted cerulean blue to match the sky.

The ensuing pandemonium, which served better than brass door chimes, brought Doña Altagracia Soto, Vda. de Morales to the door to greet her comadre and best friend. She stood smiling in anticipation in the frame of the entryway, which was embellished with cotton balls to ward off flies, a picture of the Holy Family to ward off Jehovahs, and a woven palm cross blessed during Semana Santa to ward off winos, banditos, hipitos, and assorted malcriados.

Doña Altagracia was dressed in mourning—the funeral of her late husband's second cousin's wife's father-in-law had been but a fortnight ago and she was still de luto, as required for the prescribed forty days. She was dressed in black from head to toe and looked like a diminutive blackbird—from the lace tapalito perched on the white bun of her hair to the ornate black satin slippers sent to her by her favorite great-grandson when he was on leave from the Navy in San Francisco's Chinatown.

Doña Amparito parked the car with a great sputtering and lurching commotion, dragged her heavy black purse the size of a small suitcase off the front seat, and, crooking it on her arm, slid out of the car. She stepped onto the porch and gave her comadre an abrazo and a dry peck on each of her weathered cheeks. "Te acompaño en tus sentimentos," she declared solemnly. "Your sorrow is my sorrow."

The two widows then walked through the threshold into the small, neat living room, and Doña Amparo made her way to her accustomed seat on the sofa, which was covered by a pink chenille bedspread. After serving her visitor a cup of café con leche and a plate of biscochitos, Doña Altagracia seated herself opposite on a doily-covered overstuffed chair that was too large for her diminutive frame.

"I've bought you some antojitos," declared Doña Amparo. "I know that when one is in mourning, one doesn't feel like cooking and hasn't much of an appetite." Then Doña Amparo ceremoniously, and with a great deal of flourish, retrieved from her purse, like the miracle of the loaves and fishes, a dozen homemade flour tortillas, still warm, a glass jar of nopalitos con chile colorado, a dozen green corn tamales, a half dozen pan de huevos, a Tupperware bowl of this summer's verdolagas swimming in melted cheese, and four giant burritos filled with carne seca and green chile.

"Sí, gracias," said Doña Altagracia, now suddenly animated. "You're right, I don't have much of an appetite. Give me a little taste of those verdolagas while they're still hot, won't you? Pass me a tortilla, please. Oh, that pan de huevo will be a perfect dessert after I finish with this burrito! Now where was I? Oh, yes. You know, I've been thinking about how difficult it is to keep the tradition of luto these days. What a disgrace! The grandchildren of el difunto, Don Tomás (que en paz descanse), came to pay their respects yesterday dressed in shorts and halter tops, and his corpse not even cold in the ground! Some of the girls attended the funeral mass in slacks or sleeveless dresses! And their heads uncovered! No one held a velorio con el cuerpo presente, and there has been no novena of the glorious mysteries of the rosary for his soul in Purgatory!" She sighed and then signed herself piously with the sign of the cross. She then closed her eyes in contemplation for a moment before she asked her comadre to pass her a tamalito.

"Es la juventud. The young people of today have no respect—they go to the dances and movies and piquiniquis and listen to the radio and all that cochino rock and roll music and watch la televisión with all those desnudos sin vergüenza before their grandfather's soul has hardly left his body!" (By this time she had polished off the verdolagas and nopalitos and began to unwrap a second tamale.) The widows sighed again, this time in unison, and recited Ave Marías as a shield against the outrages of the modern world.

"Hablando de televisión," Doña Altagracia interjected

coyly after a respectful amount of silence had been observed. "What can you tell me about the telenovela *María Victoria*? I've missed a whole week's worth of episodes because of the sacrifices that I have had to make for the whole family for the sake of the luto." She eyed the army of saints standing at attention on her home altar to see if there was a hint of disapproval at her minor infraction of the rules of mourning. The eyes of the statues stared glassily, disinterested, intent on the latest supplications for the soul of the dearly departed Don Tomás.

Doña Amparo smoothed her skirt, crossed her legs modestly at the ankles, and resettled her ample frame into a deep soft spot in the sofa. "Well!" she declared breathlessly in Spanglish, "You'll never believe what has happened since last week. Es increíble." Her hands fluttered like lovebirds with excitement. La bella María Victoria de León jilted the man she didn't really love—it was a wedding arranged by two powerful rich families—at the altar. She is kidnapped, still in her wedding dress by an americano who claims he has been hired by her one and only true love, the poor vaquero Estéban Herrera. He is, as you may or may not recall, the handsome and good but poor son of a humble ranchero, and at the very moment that María Victoria has been kidnapped, Estéban is imprisoned in Sinaloa because he has been mistaken for the wicked mafioso Daniel "La Piña" Vásquez. And Doña Pomposa, María Victoria's sainted mother, has been in a coma for a week del susto, and there is a poor indio from Tepoztlán who is looking for his godson Estéban because he has won la lotería and will now be richer than even el presidente de México and no one will listen to el pobre indio Don Victoriano and they are going to put him in an insane asylum because the only language he can speak is Nahuatl and no one understands him."

Doña Amparo's monologue was punctuated by disbelieving gasps from Doña Altagracia—"Jesús, María y José! Ay, Dios, Santo de mi vida! Bendito sea Dios! No lo creo!"—as she fanned herself vigorously with her apron.

The eyes of the black-and-white Felix the Cat kitchen clock spun, the tail wagged, and the clock chimed twelve noon. Doña Amparo, ever vigilant of the time, came to attention, shouldered her still heavy purse, and rose from the deep sofa with a little grunt. "Bueno, comadre, ya me voy. I don't want to miss the next episode of *María Victoria* at one o'clock, but I'll be back in a day or so to fill you in."

"Andale, pues, y muchísimas gracias." Doña Altagracia got up from the chair and shuffled to the doorway to see her friend out.

Doña Amparo lumbered out onto the porch, being careful not to slam the screen door behind her. As she stepped out into the yard, the pandemonium in the corral began again, this time with the added commotion of the young pullets arguing over the embedded bullet, which they have mistaken for a fat worm.

And Doña Altagracia, having seen her friend safely off, listing in her vintage Chevy down the dusty lane, returned to the sala and gathered up the dishware, which she placed in the sink of her immaculate kitchen. She then returned to the sala and placed a candle on her already overcrowded and overpopulated home altar and said her prayers to El Santo Niño de Atocha, the patron saint of pilgrims and wanderers; and to San Antonio, the patron saint of lovers and lost things; and to San Judas, the patron saint of lost causes—with the fervent hope that María Victoria will get

her man, that Estéban will be reunited with his true love,
that the jilted patrón will go to the monastery, that Doña
Pomposa will revive and come to her senses, and that the
valiant Indian will find his long-lost grandson and that with
the money from the lotería they will move the whole family
to a great and prosperous hacienda and live happily ever
after en el Valle de Tepoztlán.

Amor Inolvidable :: Unforgettable Love

AMOR ETERNO

Juan Gabriel

Tú eres la tristeza de mis ojos
Que lloran en silencio por su adiós
Te veo en el espejo y no mi rostro
El tiempo que he sufrido por tu adiós
Obligo aunque te olvide el pensamiento
Pues siempre estoy en el ayer
Prefiero estar dormida que despierta
Que tanto que me duele que no estes.
Como quisiera, ah,
Que tu vivieras
Que tus ojitos
Jamás se hubieran cerrado nunca
Y estar mirándolos
Amor eterno
E inolvidable
Tarde o temprano
Estaré contigo
Para seguir amándonos.

Amor Inolvidable :: Unforgettable Love

The following notice appeared in the obituary column of Tucson's daily newspaper on August 21, 1991:

> En memoria de Don
> Agustín Telles González,
> 1900–1971

Querido Esposo:
  Nos ha dejado un espacio vacio con su partida desde hace veinte años. Pero al pesar del dolor tan grande que siento, doy gracias al Señor Todopoderoso por haberme prestado la vida tan hermosa a su lado. Al recordar el pasado, una sonrisa llega a mi cara: su companía tan hermosa; sus pláticas tan interesantes; sus bromas tan chistosas; su ayuda tan graciosa. Especialmente sus consejos que tanto nos ayudaron a seguir en esta vida tan dolorosa.

Son los recuerdos que guardo entre mi corazón. Y al pesar de su partida, se que allá de lo alto del cielo, me siguen los pasos y aunque me veo en problemas no encuentro el fracaso. Me sigue guiando por bueno camino. Por eso fué Ud. un esposo ejemplar para todos sus conocidos.

Su esposa, Jacinta

Beloved Husband:

Your departure twenty years ago left me with a great emptiness. But in spite of the great sorrow I feel, I am grateful to the Almighty for the gift of having you at my side for all those wonderful years. When I think about the past, a smile comes to my lips. I recall your wonderful company; your interesting conversations; your funny jokes; your gracious willingness to always be of help. These are the memories that I always carry in my heart. And in spite of your absence, I know from your place in heaven you continue to guide me in this vale of tears. This is why you were such an exemplary husband to all those who knew you.

Your wife, Jacinta

There still stands a historical and venerable house on a corner lot in Barrio Libre—it is a third of a block long and is now divided into apartments. It is almost a century old—constructed of stuccoed mud adobe with walls a foot thick—Sonoran style—with a flat roof and a plain facade. It is the soft green color of an agave that has been washed by a summer rain. Shading the doorway of the entrance to the main residence is a gnarled piocha tree that in the spring droops with fragrant clusters of lavender flowers, and in the fall with marble-sized berries the pale yellow of the October sun. It is the only tree on that block, for the once proud neighborhood of stalwart Mexican American pioneer families is triste now—most of the aged residents have died or moved away. The neighborhood is now dominated by empty lots strewn with rubble and weeds, deteriorating and boarded up houses, frequented by transients who pass the day sitting on the broken stoops and porches and drinking cheap wine out of bottles wrapped in paper bags.

I knock on the weathered wooden door. Glued to a small windowpane is a poster with a picture of La Virgen de Guadalupe and the gentle admonishment: "Este hogar es católico. No se permite propaganda protestante."

There is no answer to my knock. I wait. I knock again. I am worried that my Nina Jacinta will not hear me over the whir of the ancient evaporative cooler in her living room. At last I hear a muffled shuffling in the zaguán. "Ay, voy," a voice says pertly, and then my great-aunt Jacinta García, viuda de González, unlocks the door with a clatter of keys and the clicks of multiple bolts.

Nina Jacinta opens the door. She smiles widely in welcome. Her bright eyes and smooth brown skin belie her ninety years. "The same age as my house," she is fond of telling me. She has done up her fine thin hair into a cap of soft white curls. Her face is brushed with the sweet scent of Coty's Air Spun Powder (medium beige). She is wearing lipstick and a hint of rouge and a loose-fitting flowered dress of blue polyester. "Buenos días de Dios, hija. Pase, pase." She greets me shyly and holds open the screen door. I step from the bright light of the stifling June heat into the cool hallway and follow her through a wide arched doorway into the sala darkened by closed venetian blinds. My eyes adjust to the diminished light of the candles of her home altar. On the tiers of the altar are arranged dozens of pictures and statues of saints; prayer books and holy cards worn from decades of use; beeswax tapers and vigil lights; flowers of every hue—fresh and dried, paper and plastic; and dozens of photographs of children, grandchildren, and great-grandchildren garbed in baptismal, graduation, prom, and wedding attire. But the centerpiece of the marvelous altar is dominated by a gold-framed sepia photograph of my Nina Jacinta and my now deceased Nino Agustín in their wedding finery. Their smiles are ethereal.

I sit on the overstuffed sofa in the aura of the altar's flames. Nina Jacinta offers me a glass of cold iced tea garnished with fresh mint. She sits opposite me in the cushioned rocking chair that was my nino's favorite. She begins to recount her wedding day in her soft and lyrical Spanish. It is a story that is oft repeated, like the nostalgic love songs from another era that are played over and over again on scratchy records, lest the heart forget the power of the words.

I listen intently to her concert, leaning forward on the couch in order to catch every word. The backs and arms of the Chesterfield sofa are covered with finely wrought doilies and scarves. She has finished her recital and notices that I am picking up a doily to admire it more closely. "Aren't they pretty?" she asks. "Oh, yes," I reply, "they are very beautiful." "Un momentito," she says.

She gets up slowly from the rocking chair and walks through the arched doorway of the living room and goes down the zaguán through a doorway leading to another room. I can hear rummaging in the adjacent bedroom.

"¿Me puedes ayudar con esta maleta?" she calls from down the hall. I follow her voice into the bedroom. She is struggling with a battered suitcase stored under the turn-of-the-century iron bed, the mattress of which is covered with a faded hand-stitched quilt with the "wedding ring" design. On the wall opposite the matrimonial bed is a rack crowded with an artful arrangement of hats—including a Southern Pacific Railroad hat—that had once belonged to my great-uncle, Don Agustín. They are still in place where he had hung them on the day of his death more than twenty years ago.

In a few minutes I am again sitting on the living-room sofa, having helped her with the suitcase which, after some difficulty with the lock, she has now opened. We are surrounded by its contents—dozens and dozens of crocheted doilies and pillow covers and dresser scarves that she has tenderly removed from the tissue paper wrap. It is as if I have been caught in an out of season snowstorm of gigantic snowflakes of fantastic designs: angels, flowers, love birds, fruit, cupids, and hearts.

"My mother crocheted most of these," she tells me proudly. "She would crochet in the evening after all the chores on our ranch in the Rincon Mountains were done. To relax. See—she crocheted this cupid as a recuerdo for Agustín and me on our wedding day. It would be seventy years this September if he were still alive. She crocheted this pillow slip with the lovebirds as a gift for our tenth anniversary. I was never good at crocheting—I preferred to embroider. I embroidered this tablecloth for my hope chest years ago, but the crocheted hem is my mother's handiwork." The tablecloth spills out of the valise, and she extends it so I can see its garden of flowers and hearts of every color of the rainbow. Last, she removes an antique wedding dress from the folds of tissue paper. It is yellowed with age and delicate as a spider web, but still intact. My nina's eyes blur with tears of nostalgia. "I wore my mother's wedding dress on my own wedding day at the cathedral. We had a beautiful mass—Amparito Carrillo sang the *Ave María*. The fiesta at the rancho was beautiful—my father and uncles barbecued three steers, and people came from all around the valley. The celebration lasted three days."

I am never mindful of the time in the presence of my nina Jacinta. The morning passes. She, as always, invites me to stay for lunch. She busies herself in her diminutive kitchen, having politely declined my offer to help. I wait in anticipation at the vintage dining table hewn from the trunks of mesquite trees. As usual, the table is set for three—the extra place setting is complete with napkin, plate, fork, spoon, knife, water glass, coffee cup, and a miniature ash tray in the shape of a sombrero.

Delicious aromas emanate from the kitchen. Nina emerges wearing her full apron and places a basket of warm gorditas on the checkered oilcloth of the table. She apologizes because arthritis prevents her from making the tortillas herself, but she assures me that she has bought them from a comadre who has cooked them on a backyard wood stove with mesquite leña, as tradition demands.

I serve myself generous helpings of savory chilaquiles simmered in pungent red chile sauce, frijoles chinitos, thrice fried and crisped to perfection, and her harvest of nopalitos marinated in olive oil and lemon juice and garnished with cilantro. For dessert there is a bowl of chilled figs. I gulp down everything ravenously. She eats her small portions delicately, slowly, glancing now and then at the empty place at the table with lowered and solemn eyes. We finish our lunch and I help gather our dishes. I pretend not to notice the unused place setting. I help wash and dry and put the dishes away in the sagging cupboards. There is a 1945 calendar from El Charro Restaurant with a painting of Popocatepetl and Ixtaccihuatl—the star-crossed Aztec lovers—hanging on the wall above the sink. We are both lost in thought as we finish the kitchen chores.

"Nina," I ask at last.

"Yes, m'hija," she answers, distracted.

"I hope that I am not being too intrusa, but there is something I have been wanting to ask you for many years."

"Sí, m'hija," she answers, alerted now.

I have been mystified for many years about the extra place setting at the table. It has been untouched for all this time. "Who is the guest that never arrives?"

"Oh, m'hija, I thought you knew. It is for your nino Agustín. I just can't bear the thought of removing it. I always think that he's about to walk through the door telling me how good dinner smells. I had already set the table for dinner the day that he died—I had made his favorite meal, carne asada—and was waiting for him to come home from work. They called me from the S.P. offices. He never came home again. He died where he fell." She took a pained breath and fingered the thin gold band on the finger of her left hand. "I miss him so much, even after all these years. Tan simpático, tan chulo y caballero. And such a good dancer." She glances towards the calendar of the Aztec lovers locked in a final passionate embrace. A faint blush rises to her cheeks. "How can I say it, m'hija. He . . . he knew how to make a woman happy."

Amor Eterno :: Eternal Love

PENA DE LOS AMORES

José Luis Almada Gallardo

Que pena de las palabras que se callaron
Y aquellas que pronunciadas están perdidas
Que pena la primavera sin flor ni canto
Que pena de algún verano sin golondrinas
Que pena de algunos versos que no se han dado
Y aquellos labios dispuestos pero escondidos
Que pena de las estrellas que se apagaron
En medio de alguna noche mal encendida.
Que pena de las promesas que se quedaron
Bailando con los recuerdos en una esquina
Que pena de los amantes que se dejaron
Sin darse siquiera un beso de despedida
Que pena de los amores que ya pasaron
Que pena de los amores que no existían
Que pena de los amores que me olvidaron
Que pena de los amores que se me olvidan.

Amor Eterno :: Eternal Love

Tucson, Arizona
September 11, 1994

Aida Romero López
Oceanside, California

Dear Cuz:

Hola Prima. This letter is long overdue. As you already know, I've been trying to organize a reunion of the Romero family for eons. It seems like we all get so busy con la vida loca and time goes by and we don't get around to the important things in life! Anyway, good news! I finally got the ball rolling and we now have set the time and place—so mark your calendar—next Fourth of July weekend at the Cottonwood Grove at the Tanque Verde Guest Ranch. (It's as close to the old homestead as we could get—everything is developed now—you wouldn't recognize it!) We haven't worked out the details—maybe you could help on one of the committees—family history, entertainment, games, food, raffle, etc. I'll keep in touch.

Sorry about your divorce, but familia is here for you. It will be great to see you, kiddo—it's been too long. Can't wait to get reacquainted with your kids—I know how fast they grow up—my boys are almost as tall as me!

It should be a great homecoming—everyone I've talked to thinks they can make it. Not too sure about our great-aunt, your godmother, Tía Jacinta. She's tenacious, but getting pretty frail. She is really looking forward to a visit with you—she is always asking about you.

Let's keep in touch.

Your favorite primo,

Eddie

P.S. I thought you might be interested in the newspaper article I'm enclosing. It's about the Pima County Parks and Recreation Program—they have this new beautification project on the Santa Cruz River—hiking trails, bike path, picnic areas, etc. You can buy a native tree—mesquite, cottonwood—and have it planted in your folks' memory—they'll put their names on a tile plaque for posterity. Thought you'd like the idea—I know you and your family spent a lot of time there when you were a kid. . . .

Damn! It was the wrong time of the day to be heading west on Congress. 5 P.M. Early July. Another record broken. My visor dangling at a useless angle. The afternoon sun shining directly on my windshield and momentarily blinding me as I wait to turn left onto Grande Avenue. The turn signal and the air conditioner on my vintage Chevrolet are on the blink as usual. I can feel the beads of sweat form on my upper lip; they pool on my forehead and run down my temples and neck. The backs of my knees and thighs stick to the cracks in the vinyl upholstery. I dangle my left arm out of the window and peer impatiently at the incoming cars barreling through the intersection trying to beat the red light.

It's been ten years—where did all the traffic come from? This is supposed to be the sleepy side of town, but I have to wait for another change of lights to make the turn south onto Mission Road. The traffic roars by and the dust and exhaust mingle, suspended and reddened by the heat of the descending sun.

Bad news crackles on the radio weather report—something about a stationary high or a lagging low, steering winds and the jet stream, orographic and convectional cooling. The bottom line—high heat and humidity, but the long-awaited monsoon season is late, with the thunderheads stuck on the Mexican border sixty miles away. It has rained farther south—I could smell it in the creosote-perfumed air, and there was a small rivulet trickling north in the Santa Cruz River as I crossed the bridge coming west. But the moisture was percolating fast through the sandy river bottom into the cold dark aquifer upon which the Sun Belt city of Tucson foundered like a vacation cruise ship of colossal proportions.

I step on the gas and make a quick left turn. The driver of the oncoming car shakes his fist at me bad-humoredly. I drive south, paralleling the desiccated floodplain of the river and skirting the brooding blue flanks of "A" Mountain, where decades of broken beer bottles tossed from the lovers' lane at the summit make it glisten like an enormous sapphire. (Local joke: "Do you know why "A" Mountain gets smaller every weekend?" "No, why?" "Because every Saturday night someone knocks off a little piece.")

When did they widen Grande to four lanes, uprooting the graceful piocha trees whose lavender and white blossoms wafted their fragrance into our open car windows in the late spring? The hierbería of the one-eyed Doña Cleofas that our grandmother Julia frequented for teas and potions, advice and neighborhood gossip, has been replaced by a Circle K. Tommy Lee's grocery store, where we stopped for giant pickles, pigs' feet, and chicharrones to engorge our already full picnic basket, is boarded up and empty now, its abandoned parking lot littered with plastic bags, aluminum cans, and fast-food wrappers. The old adobe houses that have survived the bulldozer's onslaught look collapsed, lonely, and deteriorated, their once lush gardens of vines and flowers now withered and overgrown with weeds.

I continue south on Grande until it merges into Mission Road at the site of the old Warner Mill. I can glimpse the towering cumulus to the south, but the air is heavy and still. Time has taken its toll on the Mission Road of my childhood: the tree-shaded lanes are gone; the gurgling acequias are gone; the milpas of the Chinese and Mexican farmers—corn, squash, melons, beans, chiles— that flowed greenly to the east like an emerald sea lapping at the shores of the city are now fields of deserted rubble where the flags of a failed condominium development flap forlornly in the wind.

Where is that spot? . . . There. There.

The needle in the compass of my heart spins and points unerringly to a venerable sycamore that struggles valiantly for life by the side of a debris-choked canal that skirts the road. The same shimmering canopy that sheltered our family so long ago has miraculously survived the urban assault of road widening, illegal dumping, and a dropping water table. The acequia is silted up now, and the huge metal irrigation pipe where the water cascaded like a miniature waterfall is flattened and twisted and buried in the dirt. A pair of vultures, as enormous and ominous as the A-10s from Davis-Monthan Air Force Base, soar in higher and wider circles above my querencia in the desert.

We'd go there on summer Sundays, when our father was not too busy or footsore from his traveling salesman job of selling store equipment—knives, butcher blocks, meat grinders and tenderizers, scales, walk-in freezers and refrigerators to the barrio grocery stores in southern Arizona: Blackie's Fish Market, Jerry's Lee Ho Market, Lee Hop's Market, National City Market, Peyron's Meat Market, the Elysian Grove.

Father and Mother would load that green woodie station wagon with baskets and bundles; towels and blankets and swimsuits; ice and watermelon; beer and Delaware Punch; chicken and potato salad; frijoles and salsa and tortillas. The three of us excited children would scramble into the back seat and after admonitions about settling down, we'd head to our private and cherished swimming hole—the Mission Road irrigation ditch where the water from an underground spring poured through a steel conduit and pooled clear and cold underneath a grove of cottonwoods and sycamores.

Our father—Fernando Lamas!—young and strong, smiling with his perfect white teeth. Our mother—Dolores Del Río!—beautiful and placid as a statue, reading in the shade in her reclining canvas chair. Our little brother, curly-headed like a cherub on my holy cards, chasing the fallen yellowed leaves of the trees that skittered like paper butterflies across the ground. My older sister, lying on her back, her face turned solemnly upward, contemplating the clouds in a cobalt sky—now an angel, now a dove, now a castle, now a cat and mouse, now a broken heart.

I am wading in the water collecting pretty pebbles in a can, watching tadpoles and dragonflies in the grasses near the bank and immersing my face in the rush of the watery spout. My father calls my name. He lifts me from the water, laughing, his arms brown and sure, his hair and face copper in the refracted afternoon light. He swings me upward toward the sky and the backlit trees. The droplets of water drip from my face and arms like the unraveled beads of a crystal rosary, reflecting and holding forever, like a heart in amber, my childhood's perfect and innocent world. He sings:

> Que llueva, que llueva,
> La Virgen de la Cueva
> Los pájaros cantan
> La luna se levanta
> Que sí, que no
> Que caiga un chaparrón
> Que sí, que no
> Le canta el labrador
>
> Let it rain, let it rain
> Virgin of the Cave
> The little birds sing,
> The moon is rising,

yes, no
Let the downpour come,
yes, no
The laborer sings.

I park my car on the shoulder of the road and scramble down the dusty bank of the canal to stand in the shade of the noble tree. Its trunk is now scarred with the hearts and arrows and prophecies and promises of long-ago lovers: Anna y Jaime, Forever; Beto and Teresa, True Love; Francisco and Emilia, Eternamente; A.A.P. and A.R.R., Fieles; Genaro and Carlota, Always. Elena y Donaldo, Siempre.

I press my face against the mottled bark of the tree and embrace its expanse with my open arms. I can feel its pulsing green heart synchronize with mine. The cicadas, which have throbbed mute and blind for seven years underground, have escaped their clay tombs and now sing their shrill and unrelenting love songs from the crown of the tree. I see the enormous black silhouette of a towering thunderhead scud along the ground, and I can feel a shift in the breeze that will bring the moisture-laden air. . . .

And I know that love, like the rain, will come again.

Source Acknowledgments

"Quizas, Quizas, Quizas," by Osvaldo Farres. Copyright © 1947 by Southern Music Publishing Co. Inc. Copyright Renewed. Used by Permission.

"Estrellita," by Manuel Ponce. Copyright © 1951 by Peer International Corporation. Copyright Renewed. International Copyright Secured. Used by Permission.

"No Me Quieras Tanto," by Rafael Hernandez. Copyright © 1949 by Peer International Corporation. Copyright Renewed. International Copyright Secured. Used by Permission.

"Amor de Madre," by Jesus Ramos. Unimusica Inc. o/ b/o: Emlasa. Lyrics reprinted by permission.

"Minifalda," © Lalo Guerrero. Lyrics reprinted by permission of Lalo Guerrero.

"Sin Un Amor," by Alfredo Gil and Chucho Navarro. Copyright © 1949 by Promotora Hispano Americana de

About the Author

Amor Eterno is Patricia Preciado Martin's third book of short stories; her earlier works were *El Milagro and Other Stories* and *Days of Plenty, Days of Want.* She has also authored two collections of oral histories, *Songs My Mother Sang to Me* and *Images and Conversations,* and a children's book, *The Legend of the Bellringer of San Agustín;* her work has been excerpted widely in anthologies and literary journals. She is a former teacher and Peace Corps volunteer who lives in Tucson with her husband, Jim, and keeps busy with writing, lecturing, and celebrating love and life with her familia and amistades.